SPACE ROGUES 3

THE BEHEMOTH JOB

JOHN WILKER

V 1.3

ISBN: 978-1-7326287-4-8

To my Wife, Nicole, who never stops believing in me.

Thank You!

INTRODUCTION

You're about to embark on yet another fun adventure!
The crew of the *Ghost* is at it again!

When you're done reading, I hope you'll take a minute to leave a
review!

OH YEAH!

COMING SOMETIME IN 2019!!

Space Rogues 4: The Horror Story Job

Visit me online at
johnwilker.com
Facebook
Goodreads

Want to be notified when I publish new stuff? Get sneak peeks and
exclusive short stories?

Get a peek at Chapter one of Space Rogues 4?

PART 1

CHAPTER I

NEWSCAST

"Good evening. I'm Mon-El Furash—"

"And I'm Gulbar' Te—" a lanky Burzzad adds, from the seat next to her.

"... and this is GNO News Time," Mon-El finishes. "The Peacekeepers have announced that they have identified the origin of the mysterious vessel known as the *Intruder*. They have not been especially forthcoming with details, but they assure us that they have dispatched a fleet to act as an early warning system."

"According to the Peacekeepers' statement," Gulbar' Te chimes in, "the early warning fleet will be constructing a long-range array, similar to Borrolo but even more specialized." The Burzzad newscaster smiles, his mouthful of perfectly flat teeth showing. "Peacekeeper Command assures us that the location from which the *Intruder* came is quite distant and poses no threat to the citizens of the GC."

Mon-El nods. "That's certainly reassuring, as the sudden appearance of the ship—combined with the destructive power it clearly exhibited—has been quite terrifying." She shudders. "On the positive side, polls show that a majority of the population of the GC overwhelmingly supports the Peacekeepers in this effort to safeguard against threats such that posed by the *Intruder*." She shakes her head. "Just imagine if there were hundreds of vessels like that one."

IT'S NOT A DOLL

"Happy Birthday to you—" The crew is gathered in the *Ghost*'s lounge, around the tiny kitchenette table. "Happy Birthday, dear Wil—"

Wil waves his hands. "Okay! We're good." The song dies down.

Gabe tilts his head to one side. His yellow optic sensors brightening. "Was our rendition of your birth song inadequate, Captain?"

"Birth song? No, that's not— You know what, never mind. Let's eat! This cake looks… well, delicious." Wil squints at the what-appears-to-be-chocolate cake in front of him. He gives Bennie some side-eye. "Plus, Bennie can't sing."

The Brailack hacker affects a stricken look. "I'll have you know my voice is quite lovely, by Brailack standards." None of the crew makes eye contact with him.

"I hope you like it. It wasn't easy finding analogs to all the ingredients," Zephyr offers, handing Wil a very military-looking knife. "Especially when I didn't know what most of the ingredients were."

Wil turns the razor-sharp blade over and examines it, before plunging it into the cake. He cuts a slice for everyone, except Gabe. Since getting a new body on the dreadnaught *Siege Perilous*, the droid has made it known that his new mouth is purely ornamental.

Without waiting, Bennie takes a huge bite of his slice. "This is good!"

Wil tuts, then takes a forkful of his own cake. He chews, then stops, then chews a bit more. Everyone is looking at him.

"Wil, do humans turn red at will?" Zephyr asks, concern on her face, the blue tinted skin on her face darkening slightly.

Wil snatches his bottle of water, gulping down half of it. In between coughs, he asks, "What—" He takes another drink, then manages: "What *is* this?" He points frantically at the cake.

"Cake?" Maxim offers, looking from Wil to Zephyr. His bright green eyes sparkling as he stares at the dessert.

"I take it one of the analogs I used for an ingredient was incorrect?" Zephyr asks, taking a bite of her own slice of cake. She makes a satisfactory-sounding noise.

Wil coughs again, pushing his plate toward the center of the table where Bennie snatches it, placing it on top of his empty plate. Wil looks at him incredulously. "How can you eat that?"

Bennie wipes his mouth on the back of his hand. "Uh, because it's delicious?"

Wil looks at Zephyr. "Sorry Zee, no offense, but a bit off the mark. I appreciate the effort, though."

She nods, lifting another forkful of cake to her mouth. "None taken. What precisely was off, if I can ask?"

Wil eyes her fork, then the platter with the remains of the cake on it. "Well, first of all, birthday cakes aren't spicy. Nor are they," he pauses, trying to find the right words. "Was there *meat* in it?"

Zephyr nods. "Ah, I see. I wasn't sure what 'vanilla' was—" she uses air quotes, "So I used ploth."

"Ploth?" Wil says, both a question and a statement. "That would explain it. Isn't ploth a fat-extract type thing? I didn't even know we had any of it onboard."

"I picked it up in a market on Trau. And yeah, it's a rendered animal fat." Zephyr looks at Wil, then Maxim, who is happily taking a second slice of the cake. The big man just shrugs.

"And the spice?" Wil presses.

Zephyr taps a finger to her chin, thinking, "Oh, I used grombo eggs," At Wil's blank stare she continues, "They're known to be spicy to some species."

Wil shudders again. "Yup, definitely going to have to put together a translation matrix if you all are going to try making any more Earth dishes. But let's move on." He rubs his hands together. "Present time!"

"I don't understand this holiday," Bennie says, passing over a small package. "You celebrate your birth, but not your name day?"

"Name Day? We name our babies the moment they're born," Wil says. "I mean, some parents are indecisive and it might take a few days, but the baby always goes home with a name."

The Brailack looks stricken. "What happens if one sibling eats another? You've wasted time naming it."

Wil stares at Bennie for a full minute, unblinking. "Dude, I never want to know any more about your life or your planet." As he unwraps the present, he mumbles, "Freak show." He lifts the lid off the small box, revealing… "A computer chip?"

Bennie nods. "Yeah. I was watching that movie you like." He snaps his fingers, as he thinks "…*Avengers*! *Avengers* is the one. Anyway, that guy with the fancy armor that talks, he inspired me. I couldn't improve the ship's personality," Everyone nods in agreement, "but I checked out the specs on your armor. This will give you a basic AI. Oh, and that fifth *Avengers* movie, it was really dark."

Wil nods. "Yeah, it wasn't as good as anyone hoped." He turns the chip over in his hand. "Thanks man, I can't wait to try it."

Maxim leans across the table. "Not sure we can top that, but here." He slides a package over to Wil, bigger than the one Bennie offered. Wil picks it up, shakes it, tilts it side to side. "What are you doing?" the big Palorian asks.

"Trying to guess what's inside," Wil grins. "That's not a thing people do?"

Zephyr chuckles. "No, they usually just open them."

"Sounds boring, but okay." Wil lifts the top of the box. "A... doll?" He lifts out what looks like an eight-inch blue bear, leaning as if looking into a window.

Zephyr takes the bear-thing from Wil, holding it up. "It's Kel." Maxim is also smiling.

Wil blinks. "Is Kel a popular character on Palor? Maybe a kid's show host, or smarmy criminal defense lawyer?" He takes the figurine back and turns it over, inspecting it from all angles.

"Kel is a totem of good fortune," Maxim replies. "Palorian pilots keep him in the cockpit or bridge of their ship. "

Wil looks up. "Oh, well that's cool! Kinda like my hula girl from my pod." He looks down at Kel. "I wonder what happened to her..."

Maxim and Zephyr exchange a look, then shrug in unison.

Gabe hands Wil a clean white envelope. "Happy birthdate, Captain."

Wil smiles. "Thanks, buddy." He opens the envelope and removes a single sheet of paper. He stares at it for a bit until Bennie finally can't take it.

"Well? What is it?"

"It's—If I'm reading this right, it's a free and clear ownership record for the *Ghost*... well, for the *Reaper*." He looks up at Gabe, who is smiling, or at least doing something close to it. Thanks to his run-in with the *Siege Perilous*, the new body can do a lot of things the old one couldn't. Things like moving his mouth into shapes like smiles, and frowns.

"How?!" Wil asks.

"During our recent trip to Xor-flaf for the Farsight Corporation, I was able to use my newfound abilities to access the GC starship registration database. You had mentioned that Bennie changed the registration data for you, to enable to you hide. I have cleaned the records, since I assume hiding is no longer needed."

Wil is beaming. "Thanks buddy, I really appreciate that! I hadn't given it much thought, but this," he holds up the paper, "well, it certainly makes doing legitimate business easier."

"Because we do so much of that," Bennie quips.

Just as Wil is about to punch Bennie in the shoulder, the computer announces: "*Incoming priority communication for Ben-Ari Vulvo.*" Everyone looks first at one another, then all eyes settle on Bennie.

He shrugs, then looks toward the ceiling. "Computer, send communication to my PADD."

"*Acknowledged,*" the ship replies.

"Why does he look up at the ceiling?" Maxim asks, as Bennie lifts a PADD off the seat next to him.

Zephyr shrugs. "It's a Wil thing."

"Hey!" Wil says, leaning over Bennie's shoulder. "Who's that?"

Bennie turns away, blocking Wil's view. "My mom, krebnack." Bennie keeps listening to the message, then puts his PADD down and calmly gets up. "We have to go to Brai."

"What's up?" Wil asks, scooting out from the table to follow Bennie, who is already heading to the bridge. The others follow suit.

"Someone has kidnapped one of my sisters."

"I didn't think you and your family were close," Maxim says. "I didn't think any Brailack was close with their brood mates or parents."

Bennie shrugs as he enters the bridge. "Generally, that's true, and for the most part I haven't thought of my folks or my brothers and sisters in years. But when stuff like this happens, it brings everyone together. Kidnappings aren't that uncommon really. It's an easy way for those with less useful skills to get by in life. I guess this is different, though." He plops down into his seat, taps some commands into his console, then looks at Wil. "Sending you coordinates."

Wil sits down and taps his own console, acknowledging the coordinates, and automatically starting to move the ship into position for the jump to FTL. "So why's this different? If it happens all the time, I mean?"

Bennie looks over. "I wasn't clear. It happens to less wealthy families all the time. This is the first time one of my family has been kidnapped, which says something about the kidnappers."

CHAPTER II

CONTRABAND

"Wil, long range sensors just picked up a Peacekeeper corvette," Zephyr announces, from her station. Turning to glance up, she adds, "Looks like it's an interdiction patrol."

"Oh yeah," Bennie says. "They patrol the entire sector."

Wil turns to his Brailack hacker, scowling. "That coulda been useful information—you know, earlier."

Bennie looks at Zephyr, as Wil runs from the bridge. "What's up his butt?"

She shakes her head. "One, I think you actually used that one right. Two, beats me." She turns back to her station, then makes to get up. "I'll see what's up."

Bennie hops down from his chair, waving her off. "No, no. You keep them busy. I'll see what Captain weirdo is doing."

"Wil!" Bennie shouts as he enters the crew lounge. It's empty. "Where are you!? Computer, where is the Captain?"

From the overhead speakers, the same voice that greeted Zephyr and Maxim aboard the *Ghost* not that long ago replies, "*The Captain is in his quarters.*" Bennie hurries into the corridor.

Banging on the door to Wil's quarters, he shouts, "Hey! What are you doing?"

The door slides open and Wil waves Bennie in. "Come help me!" Next to the bed are what look like two dozen fist-sized blue crystals.

Bennie points. "Is that...?"

"Trillorium? Yup, lots of it." Wil holds up one of the crystals.

Bennie walks over to the pile. "Sweet boneless zipzap," he whispers, taking in the dozens of crystals, "Where, how—"

"Does that matter?" Wil interrupts.

"I mean, yeah, it kinda does." Bennie looks his friend in the eyes. "These are... blood." He shudders. "And worth a fortune."

"I know what Trillorium is," Wil growls.

Bennie is still looking at him. "Then you know they're incredibly illegal, right?"

In answer, Wil only points to a medium-sized cargo container, which is already a quarter full of the crystals. Bennie kneels, taking the crystal Wil is holding out and placing it inside. Each time he turns to take a crystal from Wil, the captain makes awkward eye contact.

"Look, I'm not trying to sell them or anything like that," Wil says at last. "I've had these for years. Once I knew what they were, I took them from Xarrix and just tossed them in this hiding place." He hands Bennie another crystal. "He'd hired me to transport a bunch of stuff for him, stuff he'd stolen from somebody—some warlord somewhere. I was being nosy during the trip, checking to see what he had in the crates, when I came across these."

He holds one up, looking at it in the light, before handing it to Bennie.

"When I saw them, I had to look up what they were. The crystalized blood of the indigenous beings of the planet Tril. Blood diamonds taken to a horrible galactic extreme. Enormous energy transfer capabilities—double that of most superconductor cables. And they can store potential energy better than most batteries."

"Sounds about right," Bennie says.

"The moment I knew where they came from, I knew Xarrix couldn't get his scaly hands on them." Wil passes Bennie the last crystal. "Come on, let's take these to the hold."

Bennie holds open the door for Wil, as he awkwardly hauls the cargo box through. "Why were they under your bed?"

"I dunno. At the time I didn't think much about it—it was only me aboard the ship. By the time you all joined me, I'd forgotten about them, for the most part." He glances down at the Brailack hacker beside him. "I'm kinda surprised you didn't find them, all the times you've snooped in my room."

Bennie tuts. "Gross. Like I'd look under your bed."

Wil just shakes his head and continues through the lounge to the hatch leading down into the cargo bay.

When they get to a corner of the hold that looks no different from the other three, Wil sets the crate down. Bennie watches with interest. Wil reaches down and presses against a floor panel, first in one section, then another. A series of clicks come from the deck plating, then a panel pops up. Wil slides it away.

Bennie stares, eyes bugging out a little. "What the wurrin is *that*? A smugglers' hold?"

Wil looks up from the now wide-open hole in the deck. "What—this? This hole in the floor you didn't know existed? What makes you think it's a smugglers' hold?" He tuts, dropping down inside the hole, which is nearly a meter deep and two wide. He gestures for Bennie to slide the crate of Trillorium crystals over.

"We'd be rich if you sold them, you know," Bennie mutters.

Wil reaches for the hacker, but misses by an inch as Bennie dodges. Instead, he settles for hurling a crystal at the irritating Brailack, who dodges again—just barely. Bennie squeaks, tripping over his own feet, landing with a thud. He scrabbles instantly for the blue crystal. "Careful! This could explode!"

Wil hops out of the smugglers' hold and grabs the crystal he just lobbed at Bennie, tossing it into the hold. "They require a tremendous amount of energy to break them. Remember, I looked them up." He slides the floor panel back into place, unseen latches click, securing it in place.

Bennie sits up, gesturing to the sealed hold. "You know, that could be useful later…"

"No touchy," Wil says, pointing to the now impossible-to-see compartment. "Seriously, touch it, and I'll float you, without a spacesuit."

Bennie makes a face. "Okay, jeez."

JUST A ROUTINE STOP

As Will and Bennie enter the bridge, Maxim looks up from his station. "What were you two doing?"

Bennie opens his mouth and is shoved into his own station by Wil.

"Nothing," Wil says. "Don't worry about it. What're the space cops doing?"

Maxim looks at Zephyr, who shrugs. He turns back to Wil. "They're pulling alongside now, actually."

Wil grunts, falling into his seat. "Great."

Zephyr is tapping her console. "We should establish a protocol for letting everyone know which transponder we are flying under. I took the call from the Peacekeepers and it caught me by surprise when they called us the '*Event Horizon*.'" She puts air quotes around the new name.

Wil shudders. "Still gives me nightmares. I'd forgotten that was the ident I picked for the *Ghost*." The *Ghost* is equipped with a very illegal mod to it's transponder, allowing the crew to change the name and registration data of the ship on the fly. "So, how's this whole getting-pulled-over thing work?"

Zephyr stares at him a moment. "Surely you've been boarded before?"

"Don't call me Shirley. And no actually, I haven't." Wil snorts at the joke only he gets.

Zephyr quirks an eyebrow. "How is that possible? Peacekeeper patrols are in most major star systems. They're as ubiquitous as… well," she thinks about it, "grum in drenhole bars."

"And how many major star systems have we visited since you all came aboard?" Wil asks, his own eyebrows raising.

Zephyr pauses, thinking. Her face scrunches a little. "Well, dren, I hadn't thought about it. We really do lurk in the crappy parts of the GC."

Wil nods. "Yeah, I tend to shy away from places where—no offense—your people and their warships congregate."

Bennie lets out a high-pitched laugh. "*Your people!*"

Maxim scowls at the Brailack from across the bridge. "What do you mean, 'your people?'"

Wil raises both hands, a palm facing Bennie and Maxim each. "Anyway, back on topic. What's one of these traffic stops like?"

Watching the exchange, Zephyr answers: "They're pretty routine really. An inspection team will come aboard, usually a mid-level centurion and a squad of enforcers. They'll scan the ship from inside and out, look under things and inside cargo crates. "

Bennie tuts. "Don't forget how the mood of the Centurion in charge determines how much of the ship they'll toss."

Zephyr scowls. "That's not—"

Bennie holds a hand up to silence the much taller Palorian woman. "Talk to the hand, sister."

Wil gasps, then starts laughing. Zephyr turns a deep shade of purple, while Maxim tries his best to stifle a laugh, fails, then lets loose a roaring belly-laugh that makes everyone turn to look at him. He looks back at them all. "What? That was funny."

Wil catches his breath. "No argument here." He looks at Maxim. "So. Can we bribe 'em?"

"Why are you asking me?"

Wil shrugs. "I dunno, I mean... you're a Peacekeeper—"

"*Ex*-Peacekeeper," Zephyr corrects.

"Fine. Ex-Peacekeeper. Didn't you ever do these patrols?"

"Well yes," Maxim says, "but never as lead Centurion." He looks over to Zephyr who shakes her head. "We were both low-level troops. We didn't get our rank until we moved to the Intelligence Directorate." After being framed, and now cleared of all charges, Maxim still prefers to clarify his employment status with the Peacekeepers. It's easy to confuse for most, as Palorians by and large are Peacekeepers, in fact no other race serves in the GC military.

Bennie chimes in: "You know you could use one of your Tri— Hey!" He ducks as the Kel figurine is hurled across the bridge, nearly hitting him in the face.

"The what?" Maxim asks. "Also, that wasn't cheap, Wil. If you don't like it, we can return it."

Before anyone can say anything else, a chime comes from the overhead speakers and the ship announces: "*Peacekeeper vessel is in position for boarding tube connection.*"

Wil turns his head to the ceiling. "Gabe, meet us at the—" He looks at Zephyr.

"Starboard."

"—the starboard airlock, please."

"On my way, Captain."

Wil takes a deep breath, letting it out in a rush. "Okay, let's get this dog and pony show started."

As Maxim and Zephyr follow him out of the bridge, Maxim asks, "What's a pony?"

Zephyr shrugs. "What's a dog?"

Wil looks over his shoulder. "And you, put my action figure back where it belongs."

Bennie makes an obscene gesture as the bridge hatch closes.

ANYTHING TO DECLARE?

With a hiss the airlock hatch opens, parting down the middle, each half sliding away. On the other side stand seven Peacekeepers, tactical armor and all. The one in front has several markings that stand out from the others.

Guess that one is in charge, Wil thinks. He bows, spreading his arms out in front of him. "Welcome aboard the *Event Horizon.*"

Zephyr leans over and whispers, "What are you doing?"

Wil straightens, looking at her out of the corner of his eye. "Nothing. What? Shut up." He turns back to the Peacekeepers. "So yeah, hi."

The lead Peacekeeper inclines his, or her head. "Permission to come aboard?" Asks a modulated voice, designed to make all Peacekeepers sound the same.

Wil nods. "Granted." He steps to the side, making room for the Peacekeeper procession to enter.

The leader turns after the other six have entered, raising her—or his—face shield. *Her, definitely a her,* Wil decides, watching her walk across the threshold of the airlock, *Guys aren't that graceful.*

"I am Centurion Turin, I'll be leading the inspection detail of your ship, Captain..."

Wil nods. "Fishburne, Laurence Fishburne." He gestures to the others. "These are some of my crew—" He points to Maxim, "Leroy Jenkins," then Zephyr, "Marsha Brady," then Gabe, "See Threepio." Even after the *Harrith Incident* Wil still prefers to keep the *Ghost* and crew under the radar as much as possible. There's no specific need for the false identities, but its fun, and habit.

The Peacekeeper Centurion frowns, taking in each member of the crew, until she settled on Max and Zephyr. "Palorians."

Zephyr answers for them both. "We are, thanks for noticing." She scowls a little for effect.

"Birth defect," Maxim adds, pointing to Zephyr's mid section. "She couldn't serve."

Turin nods, then looks up at Maxim. "And you?"

The big Palorian turns away, affecting embarrassment. "Discharged, wounded in action, combat trauma."

Turin turns to Wil. "Quite the band of misfits you have here, Captain Fishburne. Is this it?"

Wil shakes his head once. "There's a Brailack on the bridge."

The Peacekeeper officer shudders. "Brailack." She says it like a curse. "Very well, we'll get started." She turns to her crew. "You three head aft and work forward. Start in the cargo hold." She gestures to the remaining three. "You, start at the bridge."

Wil looks up at Gabe. "Can you escort team two to the cargo bay?"

"Of course." The tall droid gestures politely. "This way, please."

As the Peacekeeper boarding party splits up, Wil and the crew fall into step with Centurion Turin and her team. She turns to Wil. "What are you? Multonae?" She looks Wil up and down.

"Human," he offers, opening the bridge hatch. "Don't worry, I'm the only one." He smiles.

"You're not supposed to be able to leave your system—" she says, then is distracted by Bennie's station. She runs a finger along one of the displays he's attached to the bulkhead, revealing something sticky looking on the finger of her glove, "This is *disgusting*."

Before Wil can say anything, Bennie pops out from under his console. "Screw you! This station is perfect!" Four pulse rifles snap up and are aiming at him. "I mean—" he starts.

"This is Tyrion." Wil says, stepping between the about-to-be-shot Brailack and the Peacekeepers. "He's a drennog."

Turin motions for her troops to lower their weapons. She walks to the opposite side of the bridge, looking at Maxim's console. "Weapons?"

Maxim activates his console. "The *Gh*—um, *Event Horizon*, is as you can see an Ankarran Raptor." He glances at Wil, his expression showing his annoyance at the fake identity.

Turin nods. "They're fine ships, even when not maintained properly." She looks askance at Wil. "I served on one briefly."

Wil gives a fixed smile, turning towards the bridge hatch. "Shall we continue the tour?" He looks at Maxim. "Max, can you hold down the fort?"

The burly ex-Peacekeeper nods. "Of course."

Wil and Zephyr escort the boarding party out of the bridge, just in time for them to hear Bennie say before the hatch closes, "Why can't I be in charge?"

CHAPTER III

RED VINES

"This is the crew lounge," Gabe explains, as he and the Peacekeepers enter from the long passage that connects the forward section of the ship to the larger main body.

The troopers make a circuit through the lounge, lifting cushions, opening cupboards. One turns to Gabe. "This looks fine. We'll move to the cargo hold now."

Gabe inclines his head toward the hatch. "That way."

"We're familiar with the layout." As a unit, the three troopers move on. Gabe follows. As he enters the cargo hold, the three troopers are descending the stairwell to the lower level, one holding a handheld scanner. "What's in the crates?" he asks, pointing to the few crates left in the largely empty space. Opposite them is the small sparring and workout area Maxim and Zephyr make use of.

"One moment, while I check the manifests." Gabe accesses the ship's computer and searches the logs. The *Ghost* recently made a delivery on Fury, so the hold is empty of paid cargo. He gestures toward a large crate in the corner of the hold. "That one is listed as *Captain's stuff, don't touch*." He gestures to a smaller crate. "That is self-sealing stem bolts."

One of the troopers taps the display on the crate. "Confirmed."

Another is standing next to the larger crate. "We should look inside this one."

Gabe nods. "Very well." He places his hand on the control panel, accessing the crate's locking mechanism and hacking it. The lid pops open with a hiss.

"What is all this dren?" the trooper asks, looking inside the crate.

Gabe leans over the top of the crate, peering inside. "I understand they call those Red Vines."

"What *are* they?" Another trooper comes over and looks inside. He lifts a round container up, turning it over. It is full of six-inch-long red tubes.

"They are a snack food," Gabe replies.

"Good?" one of the Peacekeepers asks.

"The Captain thinks so." Gabe reaches over and plucks the container from the troopers' hand, placing it back in the crate. "I believe the contents of this crate are all items from the Captain's home world." He reaches over to replace the lid.

The third trooper, who has until now remained quiet, is in the opposite corner of the hold. "I'm getting a weird reading over here."

Gabe and the other two Peacekeepers join him. "So, what's over here?" one asks.

Gabe shrugs and looks around. This movement is entirely for show—his sensors have already swept the entire cargo hold. "I do not see anything." He looks at the floor. "I have access to the ship's computer, there is nothing here." He turns back to the first trooper. "What is it you detect?"

The trooper turns his scanner around so that Gabe and his colleagues can see the screen. "Not real sure. The readers are… weird."

"I can ask the Captain, if you'd like. However, according to the ship's internal sensors, what you are likely detecting are several power conduits that power the sub-light engines. One appears to have a phase imbalance." Gabe gestures to the deck plating to his left. "It runs through here."

One of the troopers looks at their own scanner, then to Gabe. "That's probably it. Let's move on to engineering."

Gabe tilts his head. "Please follow me. I think you will find the engineering space impressive."

"You're a Peacekeeper engineering bot, so I'd expect nothing less," the third trooper says.

Gabe grimaces, but says nothing, closing the hatch to the cargo hold behind him.

BETTER HOMES AND LIVING QUARTERS

"This is your room?" Centurion Turin asks, as her team enters Wil's quarters.

Pushing past them, Wil kicks a grum bottle quickly under the bed. "What do you mean?" He glances around, then rushes over to push a magazine under a data PADD.

"It's a glab sty," Turin mutters as she walks over the closet, to poke at a shirt.

Wil looks at Zephyr. "What's a 'glab'?"

Trying to stifle a laugh, Zephyr replies: "You know... six legs, foul smelling, three tails."

Wil snaps his fingers. "*That's* what those things are called? I'll be." Remembering a job he did for Xarrix some time ago, transporting the annoying and disgusting creatures. Turning to Turin, he adds, "Offense taken. Those things are disgusting. I had a hold full of them once, so gross."

Turin says nothing, instead focusing on the small closet in the corner.

One Peacekeeper lifts Wil's mattress. "Nothing."

Zephyr leans in to Wil and whispers, "Is there anything, anywhere, we should know about? You know, before they find it?"

Wil shrugs. "Nope, why do you ask?"

Zephyr shrugs. "Because you're you."

Wil raises his voice. "You guys done in here? It's not that big of a space."

Turin looks around one last time, then motions for her troopers to follow her out of the room.

"Marsha and Leroy's room is across the hall," Will says. "I'll show you the way."

MAXIM AND BENNIE ARE WATCHING THE TWO INSPECTION TEAMS ON the main display. Maxim looks over at Bennie. "You know, I don't remember these being so invasive." On the screen, Wil, Zephyr and their group of Peacekeepers are in the room he shares with Zephyr, looking through their closet.

Bennie tuts. "This? I've seen Peacekeepers rip panels off the wall if they think it's worth their time."

"Really?" Maxim asks.

"Sure. You and Zephyr were on some of these inspections, right? You didn't do this kind of stuff?" Bennie looks doubtful.

"No, the ship they assigned me to was in the Gipsyl system. We'd board a freighter, look around for anything out of place, and then leave. It usually took longer to board the ships than it did to search them."

"Ah, well," Bennie says, "welcome to a system that isn't at the ass end of nowhere. Brai is one of the top twenty most prosperous systems in the GC. Smuggling is a big problem that my people pay yours to keep under control."

Maxim glowers at the hacker then turns back to the main display, grumbling under his breath, "My people."

"What's that?" Bennie asks.

"Nothing." Maxim points to the screen. "Lets see what they find in your room."

Bennie chuckles. "As if I'd hide my contraband in *my* quarters."

"What?"

"W‍HAT IS THAT SMELL?" T‍URIN ASKS, ENTERING B‍ENNIE'S quarters.

"This is Tyrion's room," Zephyr remarks. "Who could say?"

Turin turns to Wil. "Captain, I take it back. Your quarters are not the most disgusting I've ever seen."

Wil smiles. "Thank you, I think."

Zephyr leans in again. "These are Peacekeepers. You saw my room—theirs are even more orderly."

Wil shrugs. "That makes sense, NASA was always kinda anal about the crew bunks back at the launch complex." He looks over at one of the troopers as they lift something out of the closet, holding it like it might bite them. Wil moves over, "Dammit Ben—er, Tyrion!" He snatches the object from the trooper. "That's mine."

The trooper turns a shiny opaque faceplate to Wil. "And what is it?"

"Oh, uh. It's a stuffed animal."

"Like a trophy?" one of the other troopers asks, coming over to look.

"No, nothing like that, it's a misleading name. It's a—well it's a —it's a toy, okay?" He holds it up for everyone to see. "His name is ALF, my mom gave him to me."

"I‍ FORGOT I‍ HAD THAT, OOPS," B‍ENNIE SAYS, WATCHING THE FEED ON the main display.

Maxim looks over again. "Do you just come and go in his quarters as you please?" He pauses, then adds, "Also, wait. How do you have access to the security feeds in our quarters?"

GOOD JOURNEYS

Once all six Peacekeepers are back at the airlock, their tour complete, the lead Peacekeeper turns to Wil. "Thank you, Captain. Sorry to have taken so much time, but your ship isn't on record as having entered the Brai sector before, so we had to be thorough."

Wil nods. "No problem, Centurion Turin, it was our pleasure." He gestures toward the airlock. "Well, hurry along now, we'd like to get underway."

The Centurion turns to Zephyr. "Good journeys," she says, inclining her head.

"And to you," Zephyr replies, matching the head movement of the other woman.

With that, the Peacekeepers file out the airlock, the inner door closing after the last one crosses the threshold. Wil reaches over and presses his palm to the control panel, closing the outer airlock door. Leaning against the corridor next to the now closed airlock, he exhales loudly, "This is why I avoid the main systems."

Over the speaker in the ceiling Maxim announces, "Peacekeeper ship is moving off, they have given us clearance to continue on to Brai."

Wil turns his head to the ceiling. "Roger that, Max. Be right there."

Zephyr chuckles. "Why do you do that?"

"Do what?"

She mimes Wil's previous motion. "Look up at the ceiling when you speak to someone over the ship's comms—or to the computer, for that matter."

"I do that all the time?"

Zephyr nods. "All, the, time."

"Huh, I don't know." Wil thinks. "Must be something I just picked up. It looks cool though, right?"

Zephyr just shakes her head, as she turns and heads for the bridge hatch around the corner.

Wil hurries after her. As the two enter the bridge he asks, "What's with the 'good journeys' thing, anyway?"

Maxim stands up from the command chair, and returns to his own station. "It's a traditional Palorian farewell. Turin said it?" He looks at Zephyr, who nods. "Interesting."

"Why is that interesting?" Bennie asks. "If it's traditional, wouldn't it have been weird if she hadn't said it?"

"It's typically reserved for those in active service to the GC," Zephyr answers. "It's not a rule or anything, though. She may have just been being polite."

Wil drops into his seat and brings the flight controls back online. "Well, at least it's over. Now let's get a move on." He turns to Zephyr as she's taking her own seat. "How long to Brai?"

"Three tocks. I'm sending you the flight details. Ship traffic is tightly controlled, both coming and going. They keep speeds to a minimum, and maintain a narrow approach corridor."

Wil nods, pulling the system chart up on the main display. "Makes sense. Looks like—what? Two hundred ships in sensor range?"

"Two hundred and twenty-nine," Zephyr replies.

Wil lets out a low whistle. "Busy place."

"I'll see if I can get us bumped up in the landing queue," Bennie offers.

"That'd be nice," Wil says. "Oh, by the way, you and me? We're gonna have a little talk about personal space." He pulls the stuffed animal out from inside his jacket.

"Oh, ha, yeah… Sorry about that…" Bennie waves both hands in front of him.

"Not, even close to good enough. First my video files, then my snacks, now my stuff. Do I even want to know what you were doing with it?"

Bennie makes a face. "Gross! Nothing, I thought it might do something or have a purpose, but then I realized it didn't and just forgot to put it back. I'm sorry."

"I doubt that very much," Maxim mutters under his breath.

CHAPTER IV

SO, THIS IS HOME?

"How many of you little drennogs live in this system, anyway?" Wil asks, as the *Ghost* passes between two massive bulk freighters, having received expedited ground clearance. Wil assumes there are a lot of expletives being thrown their way as he moves the *Ghost* between ships waiting their turn to land or dock with one of the over a dozen space stations that orbit Brai.

Zephyr looks up from her station. "They have cleared us to the planet, a spaceport in Pooraj." She looks down at her station again. "I have the coordinates. Sending them to you now, Wil."

Bennie spins his chair around. "One, grolack off. Two, do you guys know anything about Brai?"

Wil and Zephyr shake their heads, but Maxim nods. "I was stationed on Orbital Station Namic for one half cycle," he says, then grimaces, "It was—different."

"A carrier I was assigned to passed through the Brai system eighteen cycles ago," Gabe offers. "We did not linger long before continuing on to Drogo Seven."

Bennie shrugs. "Okay, so that's a no then. Pooraj is the capitol of the planet. It's really three cities that over centuries grew so big they merged, into the largest city on Brai. My folks live in an estate

on the edge of Green space Twelve." He pauses. "They're rich, my
parents. Like very, *very* rich. Most Brailack breed frequently, having
large broods. My parents were too busy for that. They had two
broods—mine and one other. The second brood are all useless
nobodies, but my brood, well I'm not the most successful of my
siblings—"

"You're a success?" Wil asks. "And how rich are we talking?"

Bennie gives him the one-finger salute before continuing. "*Very*.
Anyway, the rest of my brood-mates have all done pretty well for
themselves. One of my sisters is a successful vid-star and musician.
Very successful. Another is an award-winning writer. You've heard
of *Mopo Hogwant?*" When Wil shakes his head, Bennie sighs. "She's
one of the richest of my brood-mates."

"Explains why she was kidnapped," Zephyr says.

Maxim nods and adds, "Good book too." Wil spares his tactical
officer a questioning look, then turns his attention back to the main
display.

"Why did your parents buck the Brailack norm of spawning
many broods?" Gabe asks.

"Because they were busy building an empire. They own a shipping company. Actually they own *the* shipping company." Bennie
gestures to the small tactical screen set off to one side of the main
display, which is currently showing the two hundred plus vessels
waiting to land or dock. "Most of those are theirs." He looks at
main display and the approaching planet, then back to Wil. "Plus
they're part of a minority that feels we may be overpopulating the
planet."

"Better late than never, I suppose," Zephyr says.

Wil is focused on the main display as the *Ghost* moves into the
upper atmosphere. He lets out a whistle. "So why'd mom call you?"

"I'm not exactly incapable, you know," Bennie protests. "I'm
quite skilled—at things, and stuff."

Gabe tilts his head to one side. "Really?"

Bennie scowls. "Fine, she knew I ran with you all. We do have news on Brai, you know. We're a GC core world, after all. She knows all about the crew of the _Ghost_."

Maxim smiles. "That makes more sense. Your mother needs us, you're just extra." He deftly dodges the PADD that sails across the bridge towards him, catching it before it strikes the bulkhead behind him.

"Okay, hold on. Atmospheric engines coming online," Wil says, as the view screen clears of clouds. The landscape ahead is a bustling metropolis, hundreds of kilometers in diameter. Four space-ports are visible, mixed in with industrial areas and parklands. The ship lurches as the sub-light engines disengage, and the atmospheric engines ignite with a loud boom the reverberates through the ship. "Would you look at that? I've never seen a city that big," Wil says, working the controls.

"Biggest. City. On the. Planet," Bennie repeats, then sighs and turns back to his console, mumbling something about *humans*. Then he adds, "I didn't think I'd ever come back here."

"By the way, Bennie, can we stick to 'siblings' from now on? 'Brood-mates' creeps me out," Wil says, guiding the ship toward their designated spaceport. "Makes me think of the final scene in *Aliens*.

Ignoring Wil, Maxim asks, "Why did you never intend to return?"

Zephyr adds, "I'd always assumed it was because your family was broke, or you were wanted for a whole slew of crimes."

"Being rich isn't all it's cracked up to be," Bennie says, not looking up from his screens.

"I wouldn't know," Maxim offers, as the *Ghost* maneuvers around the space port, slowly lowering to approach their designated landing pad.

"Is that a crowd?" Wil asks.

WARM WELCOME

"This is different," Wil says, as he guides the *Ghost* onto a landing pad in a part of the spaceport obviously designated for much nicer ships and personal yachts.

Bennie smirks. "Like I said, rich family. We don't park in the outskirts."

Zephyr turns from her station. "We're cleared through customs, and got a kind of oddly warm welcome message. You might be worth more than I thought, Bennie."

"Hilarious. Come on, let's go get the party over with."

Wil looks over to the small greenish hacker. "Party?"

"Just wait," Bennie says as he leaves the bridge.

Zephyr turns back to her station, then frowns, and looks at Maxim. "The spaceport controller just asked if anyone aboard has any allergies they should be aware of."

"Weird," Maxim says.

Wil jumps out of his seat, quickly securing his station. "Well, come on! Free food is free food."

As Wil leaves the bridge, Maxim looks at Zephyr. "He's clearly never eaten Brailack food before. This should be interesting." He chuckles and offers his hand. She takes it and they head out of the bridge.

As the cargo ramp lowers, Wil exclaims, "What the hell is that smell?" He pulls the collar of his brown duster up to cover his nose, to no avail.

Bennie looks up at him. "What're you talking about?"

Wil looks at Bennie, then the rest of the crew and again back to Bennie. "Really? You don't smell that?"

Zephyr shakes her head, and Maxim shrugs. Gabe offers, "My nose is cosmetic. It does not process olfactory information."

Bennie grimaces. "No one needs to know that."

Wil, pinching his nose. "Agreed. Okay, well guess it's something only I can smell, lucky me. Let's go."

Bennie rests a hand on Wil's forearm, stopping him. "Just remember. This won't be a great example of Brailack society. My family is... sorta unique."

Wil is about to say something, when "Ben-Ari!" is shouted so loudly from somewhere nearby that he jumps.

Bennie frowns, and trots down the ramp. At the bottom, a small crowd seems to have materialized out of nowhere.

"What the—how did they just appear? We were standing right here," Wil stammers. He looks around. "Are there tunnels?"

At the bottom of the ramp, the group of thirty or so Brailack are chattering to each other, to Bennie, and seemingly to anyone who glances at them, which now includes Maxim, Zephyr, Wil and Gabe.

Bennie, at the center of the mass of short beings, waves one arm, causing the crowd to part and allow the crew to make their way to him. He is standing next to two other Brailack; the male is in what looks like a business suit to Wil, the kind a toddler wears to church. The female—Bennie's mom presumably—is in a voluminous muumuu. Bennie disentangles himself from the two just long enough to make some introductions.

"It's a pleasure to meet you, mister and missus... Uh, Vulvo," Wil says.

"So, you're the human," Bennie's dad says. "I thought you'd be more imposing, and less pink. Oh, and you can call me Carr-Ari."

Wil blushes a little. "Well, I mean there isn't a lot of natural light on the *Ghost*. It's hard to keep a tan..."

"Oh, look at it. I think it's cute," Bennie's mom chimes in, taking Wil's hand.

Wil splutters. "It?"

Bennie turns the conversation as quickly as he can. "Okay, well, let's get the party over with."

"It?" Wil repeats.

Zephyr puts her hand on Wil's shoulder. "Calm down."

Bennie spends what feels to Wil like forever introducing the rest of the welcoming party, all thirty of them. By the time Wil gets to the last introduction, he's forgotten the first name. That job done, Bennie leads the rest of the crew and the massive entourage out of the spaceport.

YOU HAVE A CASTLE?

The main hall of the Vulvo estate is as big as a football field. Several hundred if not a thousand Brailack are jammed inside. At the center of it all, a table twenty feet long is occupied by the crew of the *Ghost* and Bennie's immediate family.

"Man, I feel like we need to have a long chat later." Wil is looking around the room. "You have literally watched my movies and read my books, and who knows what else in my private data store, not to mention whatever you put ALF through, and none of us knew your folks had a freaking *castle?*" He grabs a goblet of something from a passing server. "Does Xarrix know?"

Bennie stops talking to one of his siblings to turn to Wil. "Well, you know, family castles don't come up all that often. Plus, you've worked with Xarrix. Has he ever shown an interest in your personal life?"

"Good point."

Maxim and Zephyr are seated opposite Wil and Bennie, surrounded by members of the Vulvo family. "Bennie," Zephyr says, "you said your family is small, but there are hundreds of Brailack in this hall. You're related to them? All of them?"

Bennie looks around. "Well, sure. I mean, not directly, they're not all broodma—siblings. Remember, my folks only had two broods. Most of these folks," he waves his hand expansively, "they're aunts, uncles and cousins. That one," he says, pointing to a Brailack not much older than himself, "that's my older brother, Wip-Ari. He's in finance, one of the smaller banks here on Brai." He points to a Brailack woman two tables away. "That's my youngest sister, Val-Lu." He pauses, then shouts: "Hey Val! What do you do again?"

"Ben-Ari, you krebnack, I manage our fleet." The woman turns back to the other relation she was speaking with, continuing her conversation.

"Oh yeah, that's right—mom and dad promoted her last cycle. It was in the newsletter. And that's cousin Mal-Duri, he must be visiting. He actually works on Palor at one of the larger banks."

From the head of the table, Carr-Ari clears his throat. The room falls silent, as every single Brailack at every single table turns to him. Wil looks down at them, disorientated. *Are we on a platform? When did that happen!? How high are we?*

"House Vulvo welcomes home one of its own. Ben-Ari, we welcome you." The old Brailack raises a glass in a gnarled little hand. "Welcome home son."

Bennie smiles. "Thanks, dad. It's good to be back."

Wil nudges him. "You said you never wanted to come back here." The Brailack hacker doesn't look at Wil.

Po-Lu, Bennie's mom, leans forward, looking directly at Bennie. "Your sister, Len-Lu, can you rescue her?"

Bennie raises both arms in an expansive gesture. "Sure. We do this kind of thing all the time, mom. What can you tell us about the kidnappers?"

"And the kidnapping," Maxim adds.

Po-Lu gathers herself. "Len-Lu had finished a press tour for her latest release. She was en route to dinner here at the compound, when her air-car was attacked and forced down in industrial zone seventeen. She was able to send a distress call before they jammed her vehicle's comms." Here she shudders, and Carr-Ari puts a hand on his wife's arm, patting it. "We notified the authorities and dispatched our security forces."

"You have your own security forces?" Wil whispers to Bennie, who waves him away.

A loud rumble comes from Wil's stomach. The table goes quiet and all eyes turn to Wil, who blushes, then grimaces a bit. He makes a *go on* motion.

Po-Lu clears her throat and continues, "Yes, well, by the time our forces and city security arrived, she was gone. We couldn't find any sign of her, her driver was dead."

"What exactly did your daughter do for a living?" Zephyr asks.

"Len-Lu was a successful vid star," Carr-Ari answers. "She has made several top grossing vids over the last several cycles." He glances around the massive room, "She is one of our most successful children."

Bennie glowers. "Just stopped an intergalactic civil war, but no big deal," he mutters. "Oh, and you know, saved the entire GC from a monster warship, wurrin-bent on eradicating all life, but sure, Len-Lu is the successful one."

Zephyr raises her hand. "Has there been a ransom demand or any communication with the kidnappers?"

Carr-Ari nods. "There has. They sent a message two days ago." He reaches in his tunic and removes a small device. Setting it on the table, he presses a button.

The device lights up and a holographic image forms slowly above it. Wil can see a young Brailack woman, clearly scared, but otherwise looking unharmed. "Mom, dad, they want forty-two million credits. They say they'll return me safely if you meet their demands." She looks off to the side, where someone is heard mumbling to her. "Oh, and they want one of your yachts." The holographic video cuts out and the device goes dark.

Carr-Ari reaches for the device, but Zephyr stops him. "May we have this? I'd like to look it over, plus I'd like to see if Gabe and Bennie can learn anything from it."

The elder Brailack nods. "of course."

"No deadline was given, or payment details," Maxim observes.

"There was a file that came with the holo-player," Po-Lu explains. "It had banking details for an account on Grapnar, and a deadline of next Biresh." She looks at them both, her expression pained, her eyes glisten as tears form. "Ben-Ari, you have to help your sister."

"We will, mom," Bennie says, looking over at Wil, who nods. "And we'll have to hurry."

CHAPTER V

RESEARCH

Walking back up the cargo ramp of the *Ghost*, Wil says, "Thoughts?"

Maxim hums. "Well, the drop off is in a remote swamp-like area on the second moon of Brai. We could set up an ambush. Luckily it's here on Brai, so unlikely they'll be able to set up their own ambush in advance."

"If they're locals, they might know the terrain enough to know if we're set up in advance," Zephyr replies.

As Gabe reaches over to close the inner cargo airlock door, he offers, "Perhaps we could—"

"A Team!" Wil shouts, then looks at Gabe. "Sorry buddy, go on."

Gabe tilts his head. "Never mind."

Maxim and Zephyr exchange a glance, then Maxim asks, "What's an *aye team*?"

Wil smiles and motions for the team to follow him. "Easier to show you."

As they head for the hatch leading to the crew lounge, Gabe's shoulder visibly slump, then he straightens as he follows the crew out of the hold.

Forty-odd minutes later, Bennie turns to Wil. "That. Was. Awesome!"

Wil beams. "Right?"

Maxim leans forward, grinning. "So what? We modify the yacht?"

"That's exactly what we do," Zephyr says. "Wil, this is a great idea. This 'A Team' of yours, they did this type of thing often?"

"Once a week, usually."

Gabe, who has been standing near the kitchenette area, chimes in, "Captain, I believe this plan to be quite sufficient. Provided the modifications to the yacht are such that outwardly it appears unchanged, it would provide an excellent platform to spring a trap from."

Wil points to Gabe. "There we have it, Gabe says it's a good plan!" Gabe tilts his head, looking at Wil, but says nothing. Wil's stomach makes a gurgling sound, causing everyone to look at him. Wil smiles weakly.

Bennie goes straight to the comms terminal in the wall. "I'll get my folks to send over the plans for the yacht. They can have it transferred wherever we want it, as well."

"I would suggest somewhere not associated with your family," Gabe offers. "In case they are being watched by the kidnappers."

Bennie nods. "Good idea—yeah, hi mom, we need you to send over the schematics for the yacht you're going to give the kidnappers, and then transfer the yacht to a spaceport we don't have any interest in." He pauses, listening. "Yes, we know what we're doing." Another pause. "If you must know, the plan is Captain Calder's— Yes, the human. No, he's quite clever sometimes." Bennie glances over at Wil. "Well, yes, his race hasn't left their solar system yet, but... Yeah, it's a good plan, trust me." A pause. "Okay, love you mom, say hi to dad."

Wil scowls. "You know it's a little insulting and a bit racist that your parents think I'm some type of trained pet or something."

Bennie shrugs. "Sorry, they tend to look down on anyone that's not Brailack."

"They didn't look down on Max or Zee," Wil counters.

"They're Peacekeepers—"

"—ex-Peacekeepers," Maxim corrects.

Bennie waves the comment off. "No one messes with Peacekeepers. But don't worry, my folks think Max and Zee are just as dumb as you." He looks at all three faces staring back at him. "No offense."

Wil gets up and starts for the hatch leading to the bridge. "So, where are we meeting the yacht? I'll get us underway."

"I sent the coordinates to your station on the bridge. Need help to get us there?" Bennie asks.

"I'm fine. Remember—I used to fly this ship solo for a long time before you all came aboard." Wil turns, and the hatch closes behind him.

"Wasn't he also in a huge depression funk and nearly drinking himself to death?" Zephyr asks, staring at the hatch.

Bennie nods. "Oh yeah, you shoulda seen him back then. Not pretty. Not that he's pretty now, that's not what I'm saying. I mean, he's okay, but—never mind." Bennie heads off quickly towards the crew quarters.

Maxim watches Bennie leave, then looks at Zephyr. "Uh, that was weird."

She nods. "No argument." She turns to Gabe. "Grab a seat, I want to watch another episode of *A Team*, see if we can get some pointers. They're clearly experts."

Gabe walks over and sits down carefully on the sofa beside Maxim. "Thank you. I concur, more research is warranted if we are to accomplish our goals."

Maxim smiles, then presses a button on the control unit for the vid screen on the wall. A voice announces, *"Ten years ago, a crack commando unit..."*

EPIC BUILD MONTAGE

"You know, I've only ever seen one other space yacht," Wil says, running his hand along the hull of the sleek craft, parked in an unused spaceport outside Pooraj. "Xarrix has one. Looks a lot like this one actually—only, you know, normal-sized. He had let me tag along once, he was having some big party for a GC council member or something."

Bennie looks at him. "Normal-sized?"

Maxim turns too. "Why do you keep calling it a 'space yacht'?" he asks, just as Zephyr says, "Xarrix entertained GC Council members?"

Wil shrugs. "I dunno, I mean, it's a yacht, for space." He looks around. "Isn't that what you call it?"

Bennie, fuming, asks again, "*Normal*-sized?"

Zephyr laughs, "No. We call them yachts. The same as we don't call starships space ships."

"But they're in space," Wil offers.

"Your world has yachts, right? Do you call them sea yachts?"

Wil blushes. "Well, no. They're just yachts."

"And ships, they're just ships, not sea ships? Your pod thing, wasn't a space pod, just a pod?"

Bennie raises his hands and turns to walk away, mumbling something.

"Well, same thing," Zephyr explains. "Drop the 'space' part."

Wil turns to follow Bennie down the lower hatch in the yacht's hull. "You guys could have said something sooner," he grumbles.

Maxim and Zephyr exchange a glance as they follow him onto the ship, Gabe in tow. They all duck to get through a hatch that only comes to chest height.

As the crew gathers in the main lounge, sitting on chairs much too small for them, Wil gestures to several large windows. "Okay, first things first, those windows—"

"—drop down armor plating," Maxim finishes.

Wil nods. "And we'll need to—"

"—add reinforcement to the maneuvering thrusters," Zephyr says.

Wil beams. "Guess you all don't need me. How many episodes did you watch, anyway?"

Bennie, who's been looking in a crawlspace under a Brailack-sized wet bar, says, "Enough to get the idea." He crawls inside and points to something. "We can splice a few blasters in right here."

"Mount them to those larger picture windows," Zephyr adds.

Wil nods to Gabe. "Come on big guy, let's go to the bridge and see what we've got to work with."

Gabe inclines his head. "Of course, Captain."

As they leave, Zephyr turns to Bennie. "Get started on the splices, we'll get started on the armor plating and blaster mounts."

"On it," Bennie says, dragging high gauge power cable into the crawl space with him.

Maxim, meanwhile, grabs some type of fruit from a bowl sitting on an end table and goes outside to get the sheeting. Zephyr grabs a fistful of likely very expensive window coverings and rips them away from the wall. Bennie pops his head out of the crawlspace he's in. "So how are things with you and strong-and-silent?"

Zephyr eyes the small hacker, his green head sticking out from the glowing hole he's in. "Why? You have designs on him?" She raises an eyebrow.

A small green hand emerges and tilts back and forth. "He's not my type. Too tall." Bennie winks, then dips back into the crawl-space, shouting behind him. "I will need power conduit soon, I'm almost done in here."

Maxim walks back in with two large sheets of metal under one arm, a roll of high conductance power conduit under the other. Seeing the bemused look on Zephyr's face, he stops. "What's going on?"

She glances at the crawlspace. "Nothing. Hand Bennie the conduit, then help me. Did you bring hinges?"

Leaning down, he tosses the coiled conduit into the hole. "Of course."

From inside the hole, they hear a yelp.

As Maxim lifts the heavy metal plate in place, Zephyr uses a small welder from the *Ghost*'s engineering space to attach it to the hinge, and the hinge to the bulkhead. Once the weld has cooled a bit, Maxim tests the hinge. "Good enough, yeah?"

"It's not like anyone will be inspecting it," she smiles.

Gabe re-enters, a heavy blaster under one arm. "I will be in bow stateroom." He looks at the armor plate that Zephyr and Maxim are working with. "That weld is acceptable."

LET'S MEET OUR KIDNAPPERS

When the modifications are complete the yacht outwardly looks no different, but on the inside it's closer to small frigate than personal pleasure craft. Wil looks around at the crew of the *Ghost*, now temporarily the crew of the *Glorious Gabber*.

"Ready?"

Zephyr nods. "Let's do this."

"The modifications seem adequate for your plan," Gabe says. "I believe we are as ready as we're likely to get." He raises a hand, an index finger pointing up. "We are also almost out of time. The kidnappers' deadline expires tomorrow. It will take us ten tocks to get to the rendezvous location."

Maxim turns and heads up the ramp. "Then let's get moving." Bennie turns and follows the massive ex-Peacekeeper.

Wil looks up at the yacht. "Eat your heart out Hannibal and B.A." Walking up the ramp, he slaps the control that closes the outer airlock door, raising the gilded ramp behind them.

Inside the small bridge, he looks at the central command station, its chair not looking like it could accommodate Wil. "Bennie, that looks more you-sized. You want to take point? It's your sister, after all."

Bennie hops into the chair, squirming a bit to get comfortable. "I could get used to this—"

"Well, don't," Wil says, heading back toward the main parlor, which has more human-friendly dimensions.

"Sensors are picking up a mid-sized freighter down there. Must be our bad guys," Zephyr says, from the small sensor station on the bridge of the Brailack yacht. They have been flying for just over nine tocks, the second moon of Brai visible in their screens.

Bennie looks over from the captain's chair. "Okay, bring us down."

Zephyr looks over at the Brailack, sitting regally in place. "Get your green ass out of that chair, and *you* do it. You know how hard it is to get out of this tiny station?"

Bennie tuts, but hops out of the chair. "No respect..."

"None!" the Palorian woman hisses, moving to activate her wristcomm. "We're setting down in a few centocks, be ready." She wriggles free of the sensor station and crouches over to the bridge exit. "You can set this thing down, right?"

"If Wil can do it, of course I can," Bennie retorts, dismissively.

As she leaves the bridge, the ship jolts to one side, causing her to stumble against the wall. "Krebnack," she mutters, taking the short ramp from the bridge to the main parlor. "Ready?"

Maxim nods. "Yes, Gabe has finished that last of the modifications."

Gabe nods. "I believe the plan is sound. The modifications, while not to my usual standard, are sufficient for this operation." He stands, as much as he with the low ceiling, and makes his way carefully to the ramp down to the cargo hold. "I will get the ransom ready."

Zephyr looks around the room. "Where's Wil?"

Maxim gestures toward a hatch, just as it slides open. Wil comes out, bent at the waist. A second later Maxim retches and turns away. "Close the door!"

"Oh gods!" Zephyr says, reaching for her nose.

Wil palms the small control, the hatch closes behind him. "I don't think Brailack food is compatible with human physiology," Wil says quietly.

Zephyr makes a gagging noise. "You think? My gods, are you okay?" She gestures back to the hatch. "I mean, jeez."

The ship lurches, then thumps, making contact with the ground of the moon.

Wil waves his hand weakly. "Yeah—probably. Let's go."

The four of make their way towards the hatch to the small yacht's cargo hold, where the crate full of credits is secured, giving the hatch to the restroom a wide berth. Maxim looks over his shoulder to Zephyr. "I don't like this part."

She nods. "If everything goes according to plan, it won't be too long of a wait."

I LOVE IT WHEN A PLAN
COMES TOGETHER

The main cargo ramp lowers, and Bennie walks out. "I don't see anyone," he mumbles into the comms stuck in his earhole. He reaches up to scratch at the small device. "This thing itches."

"Would you rather the kidnappers see your wristcomm and cut off your arm?" Wil asks.

Bennie gasps. "They wouldn't—"

"Worth the risk?"

Bennie drops his hand to his side and walks down the ramp, towards the unnamed freighter sitting a few hundred meters away.

Wil glances at Gabe. "You good with this?"

Gabe smiles, something his old body couldn't do. It is still strange for Wil to see. "Of course, Captain." He reaches over and confirms the status of the crate's systems.

"Here they come," Bennie reports.

Wil peeks around the edge of the cargo hold door. "—the hell!" he exclaims. Further downrange, Bennie jumps slightly at the outburst.

"What's wrong?" Zephyr asks, from her hiding place.

"It's a fucking bear-spider-thing... three of them!" Wil makes a high-pitched sound. "Like the top of a bear, but with a huge spider body—legs and all."

"Xelurians?" Maxim asks.

"Maybe," Zephyr replies. "What's a bear? Or a spider, for that matter?"

"They're Xelurians," Bennie says through gritted teeth. "Please shut up now."

"Xelurians are carnivores," Zephyr whispers to Wil. "They've been rumored to eat sentients from systems near their home star, just beyond the edge of the GC."

"Eat them?" Wil hisses.

"Well before the Brailack entered the CG, they fought with the Xelurians almost constantly. I've heard Xelurians found them to be quite delicious."

The lead Xelurian has stopped in front of Bennie. Its long spider-like limbs lower it so that it's only a half meter over him. "You have the money?" It looks over Bennie to the yacht beyond. "That is a nice ship."

Bennie looks up at the snarling, bear-like face. "It's on the ship. Where's my sister?"

"She's on our ship."

"Well?" Bennie asks, trying his best to not shake.

The first Xelurian snarls, two of its legs twitching, making a clicking sound against the rock. "We require proof. We're not stupid."

"Okay, those two can board and inspect the payment, but—" he is stammering, Wil notices, "—but it stays aboard the yacht."

"You seem nervous, tiny morsel" the Xelurian chuckles, it's large incisor teeth dripping with saliva. It gestures to its companions, who march off toward the yacht, their legs clicking on the rocks as they walk.

"Nervous?" Bennie croaks, adjusting his collar. "What? No! You're nervous!"

"Why would I be nervous?" the lead Xelurian asks, squinting at Bennie, baring its large incisors in the process.

"Here they come!" Wil says, scampering back out of the small cargo hold up the ramp toward the parlor, closing the hatch behind him.

"Welcome," Gabe says, from next to the cargo crate. "I am GB—"

"We don't care!" snarls what might be a female Xelurian, based on the pieces of fabric hanging off the creature's massive furry top half. It pulls a scanner out of a pouch attached to its spider-like torso.

"Very well then," Gabe says, taking a step away from the crate.

"What are y—" the second Xelurian starts to ask, when the crate's lid explodes upward, its sides falling away to expose two armored Peacekeepers, pulse rifles in hand, infiltration armor fully powered-up.

"What is happening!" the lead Xelurian asks, turning to face Bennie—or at least where Bennie was a second ago. He is already running a fast as he can towards the yacht. "Why you little—" the Xelurian roars, rearing back on its multi-jointed spider legs, before charging after Bennie.

Maxim and Zephyr make quick work of their targets, each now sporting a few new holes in their bodies, all smoking. "We're clear down here," Zephyr says, kicking one of the dead Xelurians out of the hold. The yacht rumbles underfoot, slowly lifting off the ground.

Wil is crammed into the pilot station, powering it up and bringing it around. On the main screen, he can see the lead Xelurian almost on top of Bennie. He reaches over to a control that is clearly not part of the original equipment—wires trail out of the underside, snaking into the deck plating below. "Here goes nothing. Bennie, down!" he shouts into his comms.

A low rumble comes from—well, Wil isn't exactly sure, but it's rumbling, a lot. From down in the parlor he hears things slamming into place. On one of the sub-screens, he can see the large blaster cannon they've mounted on the bow moving into position, as well as the two medium-sized blasters mounted behind the lounge picture windows. "Oh yeah!" he shouts. What used to be the forward luxury stateroom is now an opening hatch to reveal a rather sizable starship-grade ion cannon.

"Shoot it!" Bennie screams. On the screen the Xelurian has stopped, tilting its abdomen towards Bennie. A thick stream of something white shoots out of the creature, smacking into Bennie, driving him to the ground.

"Jesus Christ!" Wil shouts.

"What's wrong?" Zephyr asks, leaning out of the cargo hold, trying to shoot at several new Xelurians who have poured out of their ship.

"It just... well... It webbed him!"

From the comms unit, they hear only, "Mmph grphllk—"

"Bennie?" Wil asks. "Shit, they're bringing their ship online. It's armed. Zephyr, Max, take out the leader!"

"On it," Maxim says. On the screen, Wil sees the two Peacekeepers leap from the cargo hold, thrusters in their suits slowing their descent.

Wil reaches over to another new control and targets the Xelurian freighter, which is now showing several blaster emplacements. "Eat ion cannon," he tells them.

PART 2

CHAPTER VI

KINGDOM OF THE SPIDERS

Sitting in the cargo hold of the modified Vulvo family yacht, Bennie growls, "I will, never, trust, another A-Team plan." He pulls some white sticky goo off his head. It looks challenging.

"Dude, you all knew about those scary-ass spider-bears. Why weren't you prepared to get slimed?" Wil's voice goes up a pitch. "More importantly, why didn't anyone *tell* me that there were spider-bears in the GC?"

"Technically, their home world is just beyond the GC border," Maxim offers, "They're not members."

Bennie grimaces as he tugs on a piece of webbing that doesn't want to let go of his forehead. "Just wait until you see their home world."

Wil shudders, mumbling, "Spider-bears."

Maxim looks over at the smoking wreckage of the Xelurian freighter, "Should have known they wouldn't bring her with them. They likely planned to kill whoever came to pay the ransom."

THEY RETURN TO BRAI AS QUICKLY AS THE YACHT CAN GET THEM there and immediately board the *Ghost*.

"I can't do it." Wil is shaking his head.

"Stop being such a baby," Zephyr chides.

On the main display, the Xelurian home world is growing larger as the *Ghost* approaches. Most industrialized worlds in Wil's experience look similar to Earth: greens and blues, white clouds. Xelur, on the other hand, is a muddy brown. Ominous gray clouds cover entire continents.

Pointing at the screen, Wil whispers, "Giant. Spider. Bears."

"We don't get paid unless we finish the job," Maxim points out.

"Which," Bennie says, "in case you've forgotten, is rescuing my sister!"

Wil waves his hand dismissively. "You have others."

"I don't understand why this is such a big deal for you," Zephyr presses.

"I don't understand how you all," Wil points at Bennie, "especially you, aren't as freaked out as I am. Spider-bears, people!" He shudders again.

"Uh, I'm not leaving the *Ghost*, so there's that," Bennie says. At a look from Maxim, he adds, "What? You guys are going to need overwatch. Xelurians aren't that sophisticated, but they're not cave dwellers, either."

"Think of the money," Zephyr says to Wil.

"Thinking of the money is the only thing keeping me from being a trembling mass under my bed."

"At least there's room under there now," Bennie offers.

"What does that mean?" Maxim asks.

"Nothing, never mind. Bennie is just being Bennie, you know—he's always saying weird shit all the time," Wil says, speaking faster than usual.

Bennie starts to reply and closes his mouth when Wil spins to face him. The small Brailack coughs, then just says, "Stealth system is holding. I'm tapping into their planetary network, to see if I can find the neighborhood the last kidnapper told us to look for."

Wil focuses on his own controls. "I'll bring us in, find me a place to set down." He looks at Maxim, then Zephyr. "You two should go suit up."

They leave the bridge just as Gabe enters. "Would you like me to come along, Captain?" the droid asks.

Wil thinks for a beat. "You know, I think so, yeah. That new body of yours is better suited to this kind of thing than your old one. That sounded weird." He pauses, then turns to his metallic friend, "Was that intentional? Getting a body that was more suited for combat and operations off the ship?"

Gabe nods, once. "After a fashion, yes. I had already come to terms with the limitations of my previous body, but in looking through the database aboard the *Siege Perilous*, I discovered this body design. It better fit my desires, one of which was being more useful on off-ship missions." The bot spreads his arms. "And here we are, as you say."

Wil smiles. "Well, good choice. I'd say go suit up, but—well, you know, no clothes. Go ahead and join Max and Zee in the armory. I'll be there once we set down."

"Very well." The tall ex-engineering bot turns and leaves the bridge.

"Hard to believe sometimes that's the same Gabe we rescued from a storage crate," Bennie says, watching the bridge hatch close.

"Tellin' me," Wil agrees.

"Yup, I knew it. I will, never, sleep again," Wil says, as he inches down the *Ghost's* cargo ramp. The ship is parked in the burnt-out remains of a massive warehouse. His combat armor is highlighting all sorts of things, tagging them, marking them as targets, and Wil isn't sure what else. "This is new."

"*Greetings, I am your combat armor's intelligent agent,*" a voice says inside his helmet, causing him to jump.

"Damnit, should have waited to install Bennie's gift. Okay, er. Hello, intelligent agent."

Maxim looks at Wil. "Really? Now?"

Wil shrugs, then continues to talk to his armor. "What do I call you?"

"What do you want to call—" the agent starts.

"Jarvis!" Wil replies, excitedly.

Zephyr has already gone ahead of them down the ramp, into the massive, deserted space. "I'm surprised there wasn't better traffic control. This world is industrialized and spacefaring." She brushes aside a mass of web that's dangling from a pillar near the ship.

Wil walks slowly over to the outer wall and peaks through a gap in the wall material. "Are we sure they didn't just steal the freighters from someone else? This place is gross and does *not* look industrialized."

"According to Galactic Commonwealth records, the Xelur—" Jarvis starts.

"Nope, nope, nope! Jarvis, new directive, only speak when spoken to," Wil says, looking back to Maxim and Zephyr, mouthing the word 'sorry'.

"Very good, sir," the intelligent agent says, sounding slightly offended.

"The Xelurians have had spaceflight almost as long as the Brailack and have a thriving economy—their penchant for eating Brailack notwithstanding," Gabe offers. "They likely have no space traffic control system due to their aggressive dislike of authority. I suspect a compromise is that the larger cities have localized air traffic control systems, while the planet as a whole does not."

Wil grunts. "Great, space libertarians."

"What's that?" Maxim asks, walking around a large pile of webbing.

"Nothing." Wil uses his wristcomm to browse through the settings for Jarvis.

As the cargo ramp begins to lift, Bennie says over the comms, "Good luck out there. Don't get eaten."

"I hate him," Wil mumbles as they walk towards the far end of the structure, where a door is half open. "Let's get this over with."

PRINCESS, CASTLE, BLAH BLAH

"Just another three blocks, then a left, then two blocks, and it's on the corner," Bennie instructs over the comms.

The team has been creeping through the shadows for five blocks already. The run-down industrial section they'd landed in has given way to more commercial and residential-looking streets.

After few more minutes of skulking, Wil asks, "That's where they live?" He is pointing at several large bulbous structures attached to a tower that's at least ten feet in diameter and he guesses two hundred and fifty feet tall. Each dwelling seems to be a series of spheres attached to one another. It reminds Wil of frogspawn in a pond.

"Were you speaking to me, sir?" Jarvis asks from the speaker in the armor's helmet. "Xelurian clans build those structures from basic materials and webbing. As they spin the web, their bodies add an extra enzyme that causes the web material to harden into a compound of similar tensile strength to Fendurrium."

Wil sighs. "No, Jarvis. That wasn't directed at you."

"It is indeed their living space," Gabe responds. "Xelurian clans build those structures from—"

Wil waves the rest of Gabe's answer short, then lets out a low whistle. "Impressive, even if it does look like frogspawn."

"Down," Maxim says from the lead position of their procession, his armor's active camouflage making him almost entirely invisible. The others all crouch low as three Xelurians walk past their hiding spot. The Xelurians appear to be out shopping, as one of them is clutching several bags of various sizes.

After a few beats, the team continue on in silence, careful to not be seen.

"According to my sensors, there are thirty beings in that structure. One is Brailack," Gabe says, from behind the dumpster they are crouched behind.

Maxim turns to Wil. "See, nothing to worry about."

Wil says nothing at first, shaking his head slowly. "Can you tell how many are in each dwelling? Also, how do we get up there?"

"Sir, was—" Jarvis starts.

"No!" Wil hisses.

Everyone stares at Wil, who just shakes his head.

"According to my scans, there is a freight elevator in the center of the tower," Gabe says. His eyes are glowing dull yellow, narrowed as if squinting. "It would seem that the Xelurians prefer to not carry larger items up to their nests themselves. It is difficult to determine from this range where the various life signs are, but I believe there are only eight in the second dwelling from the top, in addition to the one Brailack."

Wil sighs. "Almost the top, of course. Okay, Max and Gabe are team one, Zephyr and I are team two. Team one goes in, secures the lift, we'll follow. Then we go up."

At his signal, Maxim and Gabe dash across the street to the base of the large tower. The first of the clan dwellings is forty feet above.

By the time Wil and Zephyr join them, Gabe has hacked the controls. Once everyone is in the lift, Gabe says, "Going up."

Wil looks up at the bot. "Maybe less Earth TV for you?"

Gabe only grins.

WHEN THE LIFT DOORS PART, WIL SEES A SCENE RIGHT OUT OF HIS nightmares: webbing is strung all over the interior of the bulbous structure. Recessed lighting casts the entire area into eerie shadow. Creatures that look like regular spiders are climbing all over the space. "What are those?" he asks, pointing.

"I believe they insects," Gabe replies.

Maxim and Zephyr activate their armor's camouflage and leave the lift, each taking a side as they scout and secure the landing. Gabe looks down at Wil, who is standing stock still. "Captain?" he says over the comms, his mouth not moving. Wil doesn't move or acknowledge him. "Captain, are you okay?" he asks, more urgent this time.

"Wil!" Zephyr hisses over the comms. "Pull yourself together."

"His heart is racing," Gabe says, who has accessed the computer in Wil's armor. "I believe he may be having a panic attack."

"After analyzing the Captain's physiology, I concur," Jarvis offers.

"I don't feel so good," Wil mumbles, not taking his eyes off the scene before him. The sound of his breathing is loud over the channel.

"This isn't good," Maxim says.

Zephyr comes back to the lift. "Gabe, stay with him. We'll get Len-Lu."

Gabe inclines his head. "Very good." He looks down at Wil, who is now quite pale and visibly soaked with sweat. "Oh, my." Re-accessing Wil's armor, he instructs it to inject a mild sedative. Wil slumps as Gabe catches him. "I have you."

"I can make the armor rigid to support him if that helps," Jarvis tells Gabe.

"It would, thank you."

"Just like old times," Maxim says, as he moves into a smaller corridor-like structure leading off the elevator landing. Zephyr is just ten paces behind him, also nearly invisible.

"Which old time would that be? I don't recall any missions to houses of horrors on monster worlds." She grins, even though he can only see her as an outline in his heads-up display.

"Well, I mean, you and I on a mission, just us. When was the last time? It was before you got the desk job—four cycles ago now? Klimtash!" he says. "It was Klimtash Seven."

Zephyr groans. "Yeah that's right. That was a dren show; bad intel, poor planning, more bad guys than expected." She crawls up some webbing toward the location Gabe has marked. "Let's hope Gabe's sensors are better than that intel was." Lifting her head to look over the edge of the entry, she ducks back down quickly. "Five," she hisses.

"That's a lot."

Zephyr climbs back down. "I didn't see Len-Lu. Maybe she's not in this chamber?"

"We're lucky these kidnappers aren't very active, no patrols or sentries," Maxim says, looking around.

"Guessing they figure no one knows where they are. As far as they know, they're just waiting for their friends to get back with a crate of money and a Brailack luxury yacht." Zephyr starts to climb further along the web to another opening. "I'm thinking we close up that entry when we're ready. Five less bad guys isn't a bad thing."

The burly ex-Peacekeeper nods. "Sounds good. I'll plant the charges."

SAVE THE PRINCESS, WIN
THE GAME

"Found her," Zephyr says. She has crawled further into the egg-sack shaped dwelling than she'd prefer. "There are three of them with her."

"I like those odds," Maxim says, lifting his armored wristcomm. "Ready?"

"Let's do this," his companion says, her armored faceplate hiding her sly grin.

Maxim taps a control on his wristcomm, and a second later they hear the muffled whump of the charges he has planted near the other chamber. Without a word, he rushes forward after Zephyr.

Pushing her way along the web material into the chamber, Zephyr immediately levels her pulse rifle at the nearest Xelurian kidnapper and opens fire. Red hot plasma rounds burn through the hulking creature's body. "One down," she says. The multi-limbed creature twitches as it hits the ground.

"Two," Maxim adds stepping over the body of a smaller— possibly juvenile— Xelurian, its body similarly smoking. He kicks a large and mean-looking rifle away from the corpse.

The third and final kidnapper is pressed against the back wall of the round chamber, the much smaller Len-Lu held in one of its massive clawed hands, bound tightly in webbing. "Stop!" it screams. In its free hand, it is carrying a large pistol.

Both ex-Peacekeepers deactivate their armor, retracting their face-shields, and step towards the remaining kidnapper. "You have one chance," Zephyr says. "Let the Brailack go, and we'll let you live."

"How did you—"

"We're not here to talk," Zephyr interrupts. "Your friends, the ones who went to the exchange location, they're dead. We killed them. We'll kill you too."

"You—you're Peacekeepers!" the kidnapper stammers.

"*Ex*-Peacekeepers," Maxim corrects.

Zephyr tuts without bothering to take her eyes from the kidnapper. "Choose. Now."

From somewhere inside the structure, she can hear roaring and the scuttling of many, many legs. The Xelurian tosses its hostage toward Maxim. Len-Lu is bound from her neck down to her toes in sticky webbing, looking like a ridiculously large maggot with a green face. Maxim catches her as gently as he can and tucks her under one arm. "Time to go." He looks back the way they came. "Gabe," he says into his wristcomm, "what's going on?"

WIL STIRS. "WHAT..?"

"I had to give you a mild sedative, Captain," Gabe explains. "I apologize. You appeared to be in the middle of a panic attack. Your armor was very cooperative."

Standing up, Wil nods. "Thanks, pal. I'm glad you've got my back." He looks around. "Where are the others?"

"I have your back too," Wil's armor chimes in. He ignores it.

"They departed seven centocks ago," Gabe says.

Wil swears. "Okay, no sense trying to catch up now—we'd likely cause more trouble than it'd be worth."

Gabe nods. "I concur. I have bypassed the tower's control system so that other residents may not summon the lift. However, that will likely draw attention eventually."

"Yeah, hopefully it's not moving day." Wil looks down the passage, just as a *whump* rumbles down its length, causing the small spider creatures to scatter. "Gross." He glances back at Gabe just as the sound of pulse-rifle fire echoes down the passage. "Get ready."

Gabe's eyes turn red, and each forearm starts to transform. His hands morph back into his arms as twin pulse-blaster barrels rise from his forearms and slide forward to where his hands had been. "The trapped Xelurians will clear the rubble shortly."

Wil whistles appreciatively at Gabe's modifications. He nods towards a section of wall. "There anything on the other side of that?"

"Besides the outside? No."

Wil turns to the webbing-turned-construction material, and fires. The material resists his pulse-rifle fire.

"As hard as Fendurrium, remember?" the bot says, then turns and opens fire with his much more powerful cannons. At first, the structure seems to be resisting the weapons fire, just as it had with Wil's rifle—but slowly cracks appear, and a slight reddish glow begins to form. A few blasts later the material loses all integrity and crumbles, falling to the ground outside with a loud crash.

Wil leans out the hole. "Well, that'll attract attention." He reaches behind him to the armored pack hidden under his brown leather duster. His hand emerges with what looks like a suction cup, which he affixes to the outside of the structure just beyond the hole Gabe has made.

From down the corridor, there's a low rumble, followed by lots of roaring. Gabe turns to Wil. "The other five Xelurians have escaped the chamber they were trapped in."

Over the comms Maxim asks, "Gabe, what's going on?"

"The spider-bears you trapped are free and on their way," Wil says. "Gotta find a different exit." He leans out the hole again. "There a window you can jump out of?"

Maxim groans at the news, then replies, "Actually, yes."

"Okay, I've got a line secured to the building. I can swing out and catch one of you."

"Uh, there are two of us." Some muffled noise comes over the comm. "Technically three," Zephyr adds.

"I can catch Zephyr. My thrusters can support her weight. The captain's repelling line is rated sufficiently to support both himself and Maxim."

Wil turns to Gabe. "Wait. You can fly?"

YIPPEE KI-YAY

"This should be interesting," Maxim says, as he looks out the now-shattered window. The surviving kidnapper is still cowering in the corner—or what would be the corner if the structure they are in wasn't more or less spherical. Turning to look down at Len-Lu, Maxim announces: "Here we go." Then he steps out the window and falls.

Len-Lu's scream is muffled by the webbing covering her mouth.

Zephyr walks to the edge of the blown-out window and turns back to the Xelurian. "I'd find a new line of work, if I were you." Then she too drops from sight.

"Go," Gabe instructs, from their own section of the structure. Wil jumps out the hole without missing a beat. Dropping into a wide swinging arc, he sails through the air until he collides with Maxim.

"Gotcha, big guy!" Wil shouts, as his armor magnetically secures itself to the big Palorian's. "Next stop, ground floor, women's lingerie, and cosmetics." The line attached to the slim pack on his back begins to rapidly unwind, making what would be a full-speed plummet to their deaths a slightly slower plummet to their only-probable-deaths.

Seconds later, Gabe launches himself out of the hole. Thrusters hidden in his calves emerge and ignite. Within seconds, he has plucked Zephyr from her free fall and is gracefully sailing to the ground. She looks up at him and grins. "Pretty slick, the flying."

"Indeed," the bot nods, his eyes now yellow again.

As Wil and Maxim pass the structure below the one they're flee-ing, Wil spies several Xelurians staring open-mouthed out the window. He waves—and at that moment the line jerks. He and Maxim look up to see two Xelurians leaning out a window, pulling on it.

"Well damn," Wil sighs, wiggling to give Maxim room to lean back and fire one-handed, while still holding the wriggling bundle that is Len-Lu. The Xelurians dodge the fire and reach for the line again. This time one manages to cut it while the other holds tight. "Double damn," Wil says, as their descent slows, countered by the upward pull of the Xelurians. He looks at Maxim. "You haven't been keeping the ability to fly from me, have you?"

"Afraid not," the big Palorian says, peppering the side of the structure with weapons fire. Below them, Gabe and Zephyr have touched down. Zephyr's voice comes over the comms: "What's going on?"

"Spider-bears, being—well, you know, spiders. They're pulling us up, faster than my line can lower us." Wil looks around. "Got a plan though."

"Kel save them," Zephyr mutters.

"Hey Jarvis, show me where to fire to shatter the window we passed by a few microtocks ago."

"Oh, you need me, do you?" Before Wil can answer, his armor continues huffily, "I've updated the HUD. You're welcome."

As they approach the window, Wil and Maxim take aim. The Xelurian family that had gawked at Wil as they dropped past is gone, likely rushing for the tower's freight elevator. "Now!" Wil shouts.

The window doesn't last long under their fire and as they near the top, both men grab the edge and pull themselves down and in, just as Jarvis detaches the repelling line from the pack on Wil's back.

"Gabe can come get you!" Zephyr shouts over the comms.

"I could probably carry the Captain," Gabe replies. "Though he has put on weight lately."

"Hey!" Wil shouts, running his hands over the midsection of his armor.

"However," Gabe continues, "Maxim masses much more than my thrusters can carry, not to mention the weight of Len-Lu. I am sorry."

"They're coming down!" Zephyr warns, just as Wil sees the first few pointy spider legs reach around the ruined frame of the window.

"Here!" Maxim yells, as he overturns what Wil assumes is a couch, propping Len-Lu behind the makeshift barricade. Both men duck for cover as the first Xelurian drops in and immediately opens fire. "They're mad," the big Palorian says dryly.

Wil pops up over the couch and opens fire, dropping two of the large aliens. He ducks back down just as a chunk of the couch explodes. "Well, this thing isn't going to last." Another piece of couch explodes, right next to Len-Lu, who resumes her muffled screaming. Leaning down to look at the terrified Brailack, Wil says, "Don't worry, we're professionals." Another chunk of couch explodes just then, causing Wil to fall backward, swearing.

"I'm sure that reassured her." Maxim stands up, his rifle on full automatic. "Let's go!" He grabs his wriggling charge, turns, and bolts further into the residence they've taken refuge in.

"God, I hope the spider-bear Brady's aren't in here somewhere," Wil says, jumping to follow his friend.

Maxim is planting the last of his charges near the opening of the room they have just left, as Wil retreats past him. "Fire in the hole!" he shouts, pressing a control on his wristcomm. The charges explode, partially collapsing the wall of the tunnel hallway, partially blocking off the entrance to the living space they've just vacated.

More weapons fire strikes the incomplete barricade from the other side, causing both men to crouch as they back towards the freight elevator in the central spine of the building. "Hey Gabe! Can you unlock the freight lift? Work with Jarvis!" Wil shouts, firing back towards the living space, which is now full of Xelurians.

"Of course, Captain," replies the bot.

"Wil, Maxim, we're starting to attract attention down here. Gabe and I are across the street behind a dumpster, but what look like civil authorities are beginning to arrive," Zephyr warns.

"Shit, that complicates things," Wil exhales, checking the charge on his weapon.

"Go up, you drennogs!" Bennie shouts over the comms.

DARING RESCUE, CHECK

The *Ghost* roars into the airspace overhead, causing Xelurians in the street to scatter. The small warship's floodlights are all on, illuminating most of the block. With the repulsor lifts at full power to keep the ship hovering in place, the noise is deafening.

Wil and Gabe emerge from a service panel at the top of the tower, Len-Lu still under Maxim's arm. "Ready when you are, Bennie!" Wil shouts into the comms.

The *Ghost* lowers itself, the cargo ramp descending at the same time. In moments, both armored men are clambering up the cargo ramp and the *Ghost* is rising free of the tower. Just as Wil is reaching to check his wristcomm and contact the remaining two members of his crew, Gabe, with Zephyr held tight against his chest, rises from below them and gently takes a step onto the ramp, his thrusters powering off. "Captain."

Wil whistles appreciatively. As all four members of the *Ghost* crew walk up the ramp as it closes, the open cargo airlock door a welcome sight.

"WE'LL WAIT FOR A TOCK TO TAKE OFF, JUST IN CASE THEY'RE looking for outbound craft," Wil says, as he spins in the pilot's chair, having relieved Bennie and moved the *Ghost* several hundred kilometers from the city in the direction of the least populated part of the planet. "Should be safe enough here. I think." The *Ghost* is sitting in what they assume is an abandoned waterfront. The remains of warehouses line what once must have been a great river, but is now only a brackish trickle in the center of the kilometers-wide riverbed. "The stealth systems should have confused any sensors they had looking for us long enough to land."

Len-Lu, now free of her web cocoon, is sitting at one of the unused bridge stations, picking bits of webbing off of her.

Bennie looks at his sister. "Yikes, that's not pleasant. Been there."

Len-Lu hops out of her chair and rushes towards him, pulling him from his seat and smothering him in a hug. "Thank you! Thank you! I thought for sure I was done for!" She turns to the others. "So you're Bee Bee's team," she smiles. "You know, you could have untied me earlier, I'm not used to being luggage." She casts a look at Maxim, who shrugs, loosening his armor.

"You get used to it. They lug me around like a handbag all the time," Bennie grouses.

"*His* team?" Wil says.

Maxim, halfway to the bridge hatch, asks, "Bee Bee?"

Bennie growls. "Lennie! I told you to never call me that!"

"Well, the bag is on the cat now, Bee Bee," Zephyr says, barely stifling a laugh.

Wil looks at her. "It's the *cat* is out of the *bag*. Why would you put a bag on a cat?"

"Why would you put one in a bag?" Maxim asks.

Zephyr shrugs. "What's a cat?"

"Anyhow…" Wil says. "Now that we've got *Lennie* safe and sound," he looks around the bridge, "let's get out of our fun-time outfits and get on our way to Brai." He follows Maxim and Zephyr through the hatch.

Len-Lu looks at the closed hatch, then back to her brother. "Quite the crew you've got, brother."

Bennie sighs. "You've no idea, sis, none."

CHAPTER VII

MISSED CONNECTIONS

Leaving Xelur proves easier than their arrival. With no space control system in place, and the bulk of Xelurian space capability limited to freighters, the *Ghost* skips the system and jumps into FTL without issue. The ruckus caused by the rescue has already died down.

"Pass the—what did you call them?" Wil asks, hand outstretched.

Maxim picks up the dish full of steaming tube-shaped things. "Bojo noodles." When Wil takes the bowl, the big Palorian reaches for the sauce and hands that over as well.

"They're delicious! Let's make sure to keep some these in the fridge at all times." Wil passes the bowl to his left, where Len-Lu is sitting, a bit closer to him than he'd prefer.

Taking the bowl, she says, "I can't thank you all enough. I thought for sure I was going to be eaten." She rests a hand on Wil's leg under the table. "You were all so brave." Her hand slides up Wil's thigh a bit.

Wil makes a strangled kind of sound, and Maxim and Zephyr exchange a look.

"I am sure I speak for everyone when I say, you are quite

welcome," Gabe replies. He inclines his head in her direction, then turns to the pan he's monitoring on the cooktop. "The main course is almost ready," he adds.

Bennie looks around, pleased. "And this time the *Ghost* isn't a smoking wreck. That's different!" When Wil doesn't immediately say something, he glances at his sister, then back at Wil, and narrows his eyes. "No," he warns, wagging a finger.

"Dude!" Wil says, scooting away from Len-Lu as much as the crowded bench will allow.

"Bee Bee! I'm an adult! So is your Captain!" Len-Lu sticks her green tongue out at her brother, as Wil tries to scoot even further away from the ex-hostage, finally pushing Bennie off the bench and standing up awkwardly.

Len-Lu makes a sad-sounding noise as she stares at Wil, then snaps at Bennie: "You ruin everything."

Wil clears his throat. "Yes, well. How about I help you with dinner, Max?"

Maxim has taken over the cooktop from Gabe. "I'm good, have a seat," he smirks, and Wil glowers.

Gabe turns to Len-Lu. "If I may ask, what did the Xelurians hope to accomplish with your kidnapping? The ransom sum, while sizable, was not so large. It would not have kept a group as large as that which we encountered flush for very long." He takes a plate from Maxim and moves to put it on the table. "Even if they had acquired your parent's yacht, given its configuration, it would not have been advantageous." He looks at Bennie and Len-Lu. "It was far too small."

The Brailack woman smiles at Wil, despite Gabe having asked the question. "The matriarch was quite chatty during my captivity, likely because she planned to eat me and any who came to pay the ransom."

"Well, that's gross," Wil interjects.

"She mentioned plans to expand her clan's influence in the Martok sector. Apparently, there was already a buyer for the yacht, and that money plus the ransom would have helped purchase an asteroid in that sector to use as a base of operations." She smiles at each member of the crew—except Bennie, whom she sticks her tongue out at—then her gaze settles on Wil again. "Did you kill her?"

"We only killed the two you saw us take out," Zephyr replies.

"Plus those who came to collect the ransom," Maxim adds.

The small Brailack woman looks down. "Then no, you didn't. She wasn't in the room, but was in the building somewhere. I'm almost certain."

"Must have been in the other room," Maxim offers.

"Maybe we got her when we fought the rest of them in that other apartment?" Wil wonders.

"At any rate, you are safe now, and it is unlikely she'll try again," Gabe says. "I suspect the losses to her clan will set them back considerably."

Len-Lu smiles. "I can't thank you enough. How can I ever repay you?"

Wil raises a hand. "No worries, your parents are paying plenty." He smiles, then ducks as Zephyr hurls a dinner-roll at him.

HOMECOMING

A few days of FTL and the crew of the *Ghost* is back in the massive dining hall of what Wil has taken to calling Castle Grayskull, much to everyone's confusion. This time the crowd at the castle is smaller—cousins of a certain level and beyond were not invited, it seems. Wil is just happy to have avoided Len-Lu's affections for the entire trip, which has been no easy task.

"The Vulvo family is once again whole, thanks to the valiant efforts of our son, Ben-Ari and his crew." Carr-Ari gestures to each member of the crew in turn, nodding to each. "Thank you."

"It was our pleasure," Wil replies. "And your payment is more than thanks eno—" Zephyr nudges him, very hard, causing him to wheeze. "It was a big payment," he moans, giving her the evil eye.

Carr-Ari coughs once. "Yes, well, please enjoy our hospitality. And rest assured, we've made up a suite for you to make use of tonight, so that you don't have to trek all the way back to the spaceport."

AS THE PARTY TO CELEBRATE LEN-LU'S RETURN RAGES ON, ZEPHYR

and Maxim slip out of the building. "Let's go for a walk, I've never seen Pooraj from the ground," Zephyr says, taking her large companion's hand.

"Well, technically you'll only see a tiny percentage of it… unless you're planning on us leaving the *Ghost* and spending the next thirty solar cycles or so walking the city," Maxim quips as they exit the Vulvo compound. "This city is enormous."

After a block or two, Zephyr breaks the companionable silence. "That was something."

Maxim grunts. "It was. If you ever tell Wil, I'll deny it, but I was just as creeped out by those Xelurians as he was. Had you ever seen one before the other day?" He shudders. "So disturbing. No amount of reading about them could have prepared me for that." He looks up at the night sky. "I know it's insensitive, but jeez, what nightmares."

Zephyr chuckles softly. "Your secret is safe with me, my love. And no, I hadn't. I mean I knew of them, same as you; I'd read the descriptions, the intel reports, but nothing can prepare you for the reality. Even when they attacked Brailack assets at the fringes, we never saw them—just blasted or chased off their ships. I mean, that webbing stuff, it was so sticky." It is her turn to shudder. "Glad it was Bennie and not us."

"Indeed," her companion agrees.

As they near a corner, she picks a direction at random, guiding them down a street lined with shops and cafes. Countless Brailack are walking along the road, shopping or stopping for a snack or a drink.

Maxim nods at one. "I didn't know they came in blue." An elderly Brailack man is sitting at a table, playing a game with a much younger female. She's the same shade of green as Bennie.

"Me either. Maybe they turn blue as they get older?" Zephyr offers.

"Can't be that, Bennie's parents are similar to him in coloring."

She grunts and nods. "True. You realize, it's amazing how little we know about other races. I mean, we each spent time in this system as Peacekeepers, but don't know much about Brailack, their society—or their enemies, for that matter."

They turn another corner, onto another street much like the last. "I guess the Peacekeepers just never shared much," Maxim offers. "It never occurred to me until we were out, but yeah, Command keeps the lower ranks in the dark on a lot of things." He gestures to an empty table at a sidewalk cafe. As Zephyr takes a seat, he eyes the chair skeptically. "Tiny little people," he grumbles, feeling the small chair bend slightly under his weight.

Zephyr watches, grinning.

A young Brailack woman comes out of the cafe, looking at her data tablet. "What can I get you?" She asks, then looks up. "Oh, my. Peacekeepers?"

Zephyr smiles. "Ex-Peacekeepers. A grum for me, please."

"Same," Maxim says, forcing a smile.

"Sure thing, big guy." The woman winks and heads back into the cafe.

"What do you think we'll do next?" Maxim asks, looking around the street. Hundreds of Brailack are coming and going, only a few casting a glance their way as they go about their business.

Zephyr tilts her head. "What you mean? Like, tomorrow?"

"Further out than that—"

The waitress returns and puts the two glasses of grum on the small table between the Palorians. "Anything else?"

Zephyr shakes her head. "No thank you."

"Actually," Maxim says. "We're curious… a little while ago, we saw an elderly Brailack man, and his skin was bluish. We didn't know Brailack came in blue."

Zephyr makes a face at her companion's choice of words.

The waitress nods. "Oh, yeah. Blue Brailack are pretty rare. They're from an island in the southern hemisphere, they rarely leave it. That old-timer must be on vacation or something."

"Why are they blue?" Zephyr asks.

"There's an enzyme in a plant that's their primary staple—eat enough of it and the pigments in the skin turn blue."

"Ah, interesting. Thank you," Maxim says.

The waitress smiles and turns to leave. Maxim watches her go then turns back to Zephyr. "I mean next as in what's next? Another mission for Farsight Corporation? More privateering for Harrith? Do you have any other friends who might need us to save the galaxy?" He quirks a smile as he says the last bit, then takes a long sip of his grum. "Oh, this is pretty good. Who'd have guessed?"

"I've heard the Brailack brew a version of grum that's better than most." Zephyr takes a sip of her own. "Oh my, you're not wrong. Wonder what they do to it? Anyhow, I don't know. I suppose once Wil and Bennie recover from the hangover they're building up to right now, we'll decide as a crew." She raises an eyebrow, "Did you have anything specific in mind?"

"Yeah. Probably," Maxim agrees, "No, not really. Just been thinking about our future. I mean the *Ghost* is a great crew and family, but no place for kids, right?"

"Children?" Zephyr sets her glass down, her blue tinted skin darkening slightly. "Odd time to bring that up?"

"Is there a good time?" Maxim counters, "We could discuss it more next time we're in a fire fight with a monster or legion of angry pirates." He grins lopsidedly.

"Calm down," Zephyr chides, "Just saying that children isn't something we've done much talking about. I was caught off guard."

Maxim looks down at his glass. "Let's get some of this to bring back to the ship." He stands up, squeezing out of the tiny chair.

Zephyr moves to follow, then rests her hand on his arm, "You know I'd raise children with you wherever we are, and they'd be amazing."

He smiles, "They would be."

THE MORNING AFTER

W il walks into the main lounge of the ridiculously opulent suite Bennie's parents have provided. The smell of cooking bacon is enough to drive him to motion, despite the raging headache he's suffering from. "Who do I have to kiss for breakfast?"

Zephyr turns from the cooktop. "Not me. You look like dren by the way."

Wil half sits, half collapses into the bench at the dining room table. "Oh, that's good, since that's how I feel. Wouldn't want to not look the part." He reaches up and rubs his temples. Zephyr lets out a laugh that makes Wil wince. "Less of that, please." He looks around the lounge area. "Where is everyone?"

"Maxim went to take a shower after getting the bacon from the *Ghost*. I have no idea where Bennie or Gabe are." She moves the bacon to a plate and joins Wil at the table. "Save some for Maxim."

Wil looks at the plate of still-sizzling bacon, and grimaces. "Not a problem." He takes two pieces and starts moving them around his plate.

"So how did the rest of the party go?" Zephyr asks, taking a piece of bacon and shoving the whole thing in her mouth. "Mmmm. Your world really is full of wonders."

Wil takes a breath. "Just the one wonder, really." He takes a bite of bacon then continues. "I don't remember a great deal about last night. I'm not even sure how I got up here." He gestures to the luxury suite they are sitting in. The lounge area is surrounded by doors leading to the several sleeping rooms.

"That was me," Gabe says, walking into the lounge from the door that leads to one of the rooms. "You and Bennie were unable to walk, so I carried you both up here and put you to bed."

"Uh, I woke up naked," Wil says, starting to blush.

"It was my understanding from Bennie that you sleep in the nude," Gabe offers, coming to stand near the table.

Zephyr stifles another laugh as Wil makes a sour-looking face. "Wait." He holds up a finger. "One, why are you Bennie discussing my sleeping habits?" He raises another finger. "Two, that doesn't mean you needed to undress me." He looks around. "God, this is nightmare fuel."

Zephyr has given up trying to control her laughter and is slapping the table repeatedly, tears in her eyes.

Gabe tilts his head. "Forgive me, Captain. I was simply attempting to make sure you were comfortable. I assure you, your privacy is paramount, I would never discuss anything I saw—"

"—you mean, like when you and Bennie chat about how I sleep?" Wil interrupts.

"That was an isolated incident, I assure you. Bennie was traumatized and needed to—"

"—traumatized? By what?" Wil is turning a shade of red that Zephyr has never seen.

"What's going on?" Maxim asks, entering the lounge.

Before Wil or Gabe can answer, Zephyr does. "Wil got super drunk, and Gabe brought him back here and undressed him, before tucking him in." She takes a bite of bacon. "Oh, and Gabe and Bennie talk about Wil sleeping naked."

"That is not!—well, I mean, technically—Jesus!" Wil says,

throwing his arms up. "Gabe, from this point forward, never, ever, undress me."

"What if—"

"Never," Wil cuts him off. His face and voice are making it clear that no further discussion is needed.

"Of course, Captain," Gabe says, inclining his head.

Maxim, who has stopped at the threshold of the lounge, is just staring at each of his crew mates in turn. He shakes himself and walks over to the table to grab a piece of bacon. Putting one hand on Wil's shoulder, he says, "Don't worry, I doubt he's seen very many. He won't have anything to compare against."

Zephyr erupts in laughter, nearly falling off the stool she's been sitting on. Wil turns an even deeper shade of red. "Fuck off!"

"I have in fact seen—" Gabe begins.

Wil levels a finger at Gabe. "One more word."

Gabe closes his mouth.

"Why are you all being so loud?" Bennie asks, walking in and rubbing his temples.

"Wil got drunk and Gabe—" Zephyr starts.

"No!" Wil shouts, then winces. Standing up, he announces: "I'm going back to that super comfy bed in my room."

MOMMA SPIDER-BEARS

"We've been cleared out of the Brai system," Zephyr reports, looking up from her station.

"Sounds good." Wil brings the *Ghost* on to a heading out of the gravity well of the planetary system. "Looks like ten centocks to FTL." He turns his chair to face Bennie's station. "So, that's your family, huh?"

Bennie looks at him, deadpan. "Yes..."

"Pretty rich," Wil adds.

"Very." Bennie hasn't taken his eyes off Wil. Maxim and Zephyr are watching intently.

"Maybe—"

"No. Whatever you were going to say, no. I don't like visiting Brai, I don't have any intentions of returning any time soon. No, whatever it is, no."

"But, dude—" Wil starts.

"No!" Bennie says, turning back to look at his myriad displays, which he stabs to punctuate his reply.

"Fine, I think it—ouch!" Wil rubs his forehead, where a red mark is forming from the data PADD that just careened off his head to clatter to the floor near the main display screen. "Asshole," he groans.

"Wil, picking up a small craft on an intercept course," Zephyr says, breaking Wil out of his thoughts of bloody revenge on Bennie. "Putting it on screen."

The main display flickers to a zoomed-in view of a small craft. A freighter possibly. "What is it?" Wil asks.

"Unknown. It's not broadcasting any identification," Zephyr replies.

"Raising shields, arming weapons," Maxim says. The lighting in the bridge shifts to a red color.

"I guess hail them. Doesn't look like they're much of a threat," Wil says, making minor adjustments to their course. The small vessel adjusts too, definitely trying to intercept them.

"Picking up power readings," Maxim warns. The small craft is now a mere two million kilometers from the *Ghost*.

"Going evasive! Zee, call your pals on that corvette, what's its name? *Enforced Peace*?, this is their job!" Wil throws the controls hard to one side, banking the *Ghost* in a tight arc, up and over from their original trajectory. The small craft continues to close in.

"Missiles!" Maxim says, slightly louder than his regular voice. The sound of the aft weapons opening firing reverberates through the ship.

"They're replying," Zephyr says, as the screen switches from the view of the attacking craft to an image that causes Wil's heart to skip a beat.

A Xelurian has appeared on screen. But where the bear-like parts of the Xelurians they've encountered up until now have all been brown or black, this one is more like a polar bear in appearance. "I will destroy you!" a decidedly female sounding voice says.

Wil glances over to Zephyr. "Must be momma spider-bear?"

"As good a guess as any," she replies as the *Ghost* lurches—one of the missiles has made it past Maxim's defensive fire.

"No damage," the tactical officer says gruffly.

"Look ma'am, we don't want trouble, and I'd hate to kill you, but you know, we will. Your clan brought this on yourselves. I mean, you had to know there was risk in kidnapping a super wealthy, super popular Brailack."

"All you had to do was pay the ransom! You've ruined us!"

"Uh, I mean, you made these choices. As my grandma used to say before whacking my hands with a stick, back on her—" At this, the Xelurian matriarch roars. "—*make better choices!*" Wil finishes. He makes a slicing motion and the screen goes back to the forward view of space that it usually shows.

"Wil, the *Enforced Peace* is en route," Zephyr reports. "We should keep evading and let them deal with it."

"Why? Maxim can blast that crazy spider-bear out of the sky, easy," Wil says, pushing the *Ghost* down and around, back towards Brai, and further into the gravity well of the planet.

"Because if we destroy that ship," Maxim answers, "Turin will have to detain us while she investigates. If she saves us from a deranged Xelurian, she'll ask a few questions and send us on our way." He adds, "more missiles incoming. That is an impressive little ship. Wonder where she got it?"

When the weapons-fire had started, the other hundred or so ships of various sizes in the area had all started to scatter. Freighters of all classes are forming a cloud of moving obstacles that Wil is moving around and behind. Luckily, most have shields enough to absorb some of the stray weapons-fire. Wil brings the *Ghost* around behind a massive bulk freighter, and accelerates the moment the Xelurians' small attack craft is blocked, putting some distance between them. The *Ghost* rocks again as another missile still manages to find them and make contact.

"*Enforced Peace* is here!" Zephyr shouts over an alarm that has started to warble from the main console in front of Wil. "Opening fire."

Wil presses a button to refocus the main display on the attacking

Xelurian matriarch, just as her ship is ripped to pieces by Peace-keeper blaster bolts. "Well that wasn't too bad."

"A bit anti-climactic, if you ask me," Bennie says from his station. He stands and stretches, before heading for the hatch leading off the bridge. "I'm getting a snack."

Wil looks at Maxim, then Zephyr. "Any other races out there that might give me nightmares? You know, so I can prepare myself."

Maxim raises his hand. "You've seen Gwaptars, right?" He shudders.

CHAPTER VIII

OLD BOSSES

As the *Ghost* approaches the edge of the gravity well of Brai, Zephyr looks up from her screen. "Uh, Wil, incoming Comm."

Wil looks up from his station. "Okay? Who is it?"

"Xarrix," Zephyr says, her disgust not well hidden.

"The fuck does he want? Fine, put him through." Wil sits up straighter in his chair.

The main display switches from the ship's diagnostic it was displaying to the familiar reptilian visage of infamous crime boss and all around horrible being, Xarrix. "The fuck do you want, lizard-face?" Wil growls at the screen.

Xarrix smirks. "Come now. You can't still be mad—"

Wil cuts him off. "You put a price on our heads, for doing a job for you."

Xarrix waves away the retort. "Oh come on. That was ages ago."

"Barely a cycle," Zephyr offers.

Xarrix squints. "Hmm, well, anyway. I have need of your services, and will pay handsomely."

"Upfront? And what services?" Wil says.

Xarrix lets loose a low growl. "Very well, upfront."

"Wil, you can't be—" Maxim starts.

Wil looks at Maxim and shakes his head almost imperceptibly. The large Palorian grimaces slightly, but closes his mouth.

"What's the job?" Wil asks.

Xarrix grins. "Excellent. The job is simple. I've been hired to put together a protection detail for a salvage operation. I had almost moved on to another contractor, by the way."

Wil rolls his hand in a "go on" motion. "And?" he says, as Bennie walks in, sandwich in one hand, water bottle in the other.

"And nothing. You and your crew have exhibited a propensity for staying alive even against incredible odds and protecting others while you do it. Don't think I haven't been following your exploits." Xarrix tilts his head. "You're a little hard to ignore."

"Because we're awesome," Bennie chimes in, balancing the water bottle precariously on the edge of his station.

Wil mouths *well done*, then turns back to Xarrix. "Okay, so what're we protecting? What are you salvaging?"

"I'll provide the details, and payment when you arrive at Fury."

"I hate Fury," Zephyr grumbles, barely under her breath.

The crime boss glances at her. "Yes well, this has been fun, I have so missed conversing with you Wil. I'm transferring details now. See you soon." He raises a scaled hand and wiggles his fingers.

When the screen goes dark, Wil turns to Maxim. "Sorry buddy. I wasn't trying to be rude, I wanted to hear him out." He turns to the others. "So, what do you think?"

"Xarrix can grolack himself," Maxim says.

"How much money?" Bennie asks.

Zephyr squints at Bennie, tutting. "Well… I *am* a little curious about the money, too." She glances at Maxim, who's glaring at her. "What? Now that we're not Peacekeepers, I've realized how much stuff costs!"

Wil nods to Zephyr. "Take a look."

She turns to her console, accessing the file that Xarrix has transmitted. She lets out a low whistle. "Wow."

Bennie leans forward in his chair. "What? How much? Come on!"

Zephyr turns to the others. "A lot. Almost a million credits."

"That's a dren-load of money," Maxim admits.

"We could fill the hold and swim around in that many credits," Bennie says, rubbing his little green hands together.

"Okay, chill out Scrooge McDuck. There will be no swimming around in our money. For one thing, I don't think it'd work. For another, that's disgusting, I don't want to touch a single credit that's been anywhere near your nethers."

"Scrooge mac-what? Nethers?" Bennie looks at Zephyr, who shakes her head, then at Maxim, who does the same.

Wil waves his hand. "Not important. Zephyr, get us cleared for departure if you wouldn't mind." Tilting his head towards the ceiling, he says, "Gabe, we're thinking of taking a job for Xarrix. Pay is kind of ridiculous, in a good way. You okay with that?"

"I have no issue with that," the ceiling replies in Gabe's voice. "Oh, and we are ready to take off at your discretion. I've completed the diagnostic I was running on the main reactor."

"You were running a diagnostic?"

"I left a message for you in your inbox."

Wil looks around the bridge; Zephyr is resting her face in her hands, Maxim is shaking his head slowly, and Bennie is snickering.

"Oh, yeah, well sure. Thanks, bud!" Wil says, scooting around in his chair to get comfortable. "Everyone ready?"

Zephyr turns. "We're cleared for departure."

Wil grabs the flight controls and slides the power control forward for the repulsor lifts. "Atmospheric engine ignition in 15 micro tocks."

SAME OLD FURY, SORTA

"Do you think we'll be able to scrounge up more XPX-1900s?" Maxim wonders aloud, looking at the planet Fury on the main screen.

"I wouldn't be surprised. If you could find them on Trull Prime, you'll probably find more current models here on Fury," Wil says.

Bennie turns in his chair. "I hope I can get my hands on some new multiplexers."

"First, we find out what the job is. No spending credits we don't have yet." Wil looks right at Bennie.

The Brailack hacker sighs. "Fine. Where are we landing anyway?"

On the main display the planet has grown, cities and spaceports now visible. Wil nods towards the screen. "Pulto."

"Never heard of it," Maxim says.

"Because it sucks," Bennie says. "There's nothing good at Pulto Spaceport. Why is Xarrix meeting us there? There isn't even a night market."

Wil shrugs. "He didn't say. What's so bad about it?" The ship shudders as it enters the atmosphere. Wil grips the flight controls, adjusting the ship's course, before glancing at Bennie. "I mean, all of Fury is kind of a shit-hole. I've been to a few of the bigger cities over the years doing drop-offs or pickups. Pulto's new to me."

Bennie makes a face. "You ain't seen nothing. Pulto is one of the older cities. You know, from when the world was being settled. Fury wasn't always the mostly lawless hellscape it is now. From what I understand, the original settlers were a religious group escaping persecution."

"Persecution from whom?" Maxim wonders. Bennie shrugs, either not knowing the answer, or not caring about the answer.

"I had no idea," Zephyr says, turning to listen more intently to Bennie. "How long did you live on Fury?"

Bennie scratches his chin. "Hmmm, I think around twelve solar cycles, maybe thirteen. I didn't pay much attention. You know, until you and the big man over there—" he gestures to Maxim, who scowls at him, "—barged in and got my workshop destroyed."

"Blame Wil, he sent us to you," Maxim offers.

"Me?" Wil says, not taking his eyes off the screen. "You should be thanking me, all three of you. I mean, two of you would likely be dead or working in a borrill mine on a Partherian penal colony, and one of you would still be living a really boring life hacking government servers and carrying out corporate espionage for hire. Definitely better, thanks to me."

"I liked boring. It paid tremendously well, and no monsters ever tried to kill me," Bennie retorts. "Anyway, the early settlers, in an effort to jumpstart their new world, were very welcoming of others; offering large swaths of land and such. Partly to boost population numbers quickly, but also to show that being closed off isn't a good idea—you know, to rub it in their persecutor's faces or something.

"Well, they were a little too welcoming, and within ten or twenty cycles there were more towns and cities populated by wildcatters, and those looking for refuge than there were the—" He rubs his head with one hand. "—what were they called?" He claps his hands once. "The Ulop, that's right. Anyway, yeah, they quickly lost control of the planet. Now they're more or less confined to Pulto.

The rest of the planet leaves them be, and they're too few to do anything to the other cities and towns."

"I'm kind of surprised they haven't been run off by the rest of the population," Maxim says.

"Can't, they're the ones that hold the colonial charter. Technically they run Fury. If they left, the GC could come in and crackdown."

"Interesting," Zephyr muses.

Wil turns slightly. "So... why is it so bad?"

Bennie smiles. "Oh yeah, that. They are hyper into their religious beliefs and tolerate zero infractions of their religious code. I guess tolerance only goes so far, and it stops dead at breaking their laws." He turns back to his console, then turns back to Wil. "Oh, and Zephyr and Maxim will have to stay aboard the ship. They aren't fans of Peacekeepers."

"Ex—" Maxim starts.

"—I know, *ex*-Peacekeepers. We can certainly stop every four steps to explain the difference, or you two can stay aboard the ship." Bennie shrugs. "Doesn't matter to me."

As the *Ghost* begins its final approach toward Pulto and its only spaceport, Zephyr looks at Maxim, then Wil. "We'll stay aboard and keep an eye on things."

Maxim nods in agreement.

Wil looks at the ceiling. "Hey Gabe, when we land, meet us in the hold, It's field trip time."

"Acknowledged," the voice of Gabe replies.

"You know you don't have to look at the ceiling to activate the ship-wide comms, right?" Maxim asks.

Wil glances sideways at Maxim. "I know, but then none of you think I'm talking to you."

"That actually makes sense," Zephyr says, smiling. "I hadn't thought of that."

"You're going to give him a big head," Bennie says, hopping

down out of his chair and walking towards the bridge hatch. "I'll be in the hold. Don't crash."

"Asshole," Wil mutters, bringing the ship down into the large, two-kilometer-wide bowl of the spaceport. Moments later, the *Ghost* sets down on its designated landing pad.

SPACE CULTS, YAY

As the *Ghost*'s cargo ramp lowers, Wil looks over at Bennie. "You all set?"

"Why wouldn't I be?" the Brailack asks, then starts off down the ramp.

The spaceport, on the surface, looks just like any other on Fury; kind of dingy, only maintained just enough to keep from being condemned, overcrowded with ships, both working and not, with aliens of all types milling around.

"Bennie, is there a market outside this spaceport? I did not see one when reviewing the sensor data," Gabe says, joining the hacker on the duracrete surface of the spaceport. Bennie wiggles one hand in the universal *so-so* gesture.

As Wil joins them, the cargo ramp raises. Over the comms, Zephyr says, "Good luck. Don't let Xarrix swindle us."

Wil tuts. "Come on, son," he says in a deeper voice than his normal one.

Bennie looks up at him. "What's that supposed to be?"

"Never mind. Come on." Wil starts off towards the exit of the spaceport.

"Wow, this is like frontier land, but with aliens," Wil says. The city beyond the walls of the spaceport is a weird mix of modern and rustic. In the distance, the main residential area is a series of mid-height towers, made of polished stone of some type. The immediate area around the port is full of wooden warehouses and commercial buildings, of various designs and levels of upkeep.

Most of the people on the street are in red velvety robes, with hoods up over their heads. Visitors stand out, a lot. "Should we procure robes?" Gabe asks.

Wil shakes his head. "No, it's probably good we stand out a bit. I'd rather look like any other visitor, than someone trying to blend in." He glances at a robed figure walking by them. "Plus those look really hot." He brushes his brown duster open, adjusting the gun belt on his hip. His heavy armor is back aboard the *Ghost*, since the likelihood of a firefight seems low—plus he hasn't entirely gotten used to Jarvis.

"So, what do these folks do? You know, when not praying and stuff," Wil asks, glancing down at Bennie, then back to the street. Small wheeled cars are bustling up and down the road, some towing small trailers.

"Farm," Bennie offers.

"What do they farm?" Gabe asks. "I was not aware of agriculture on Fury."

"Goju."

"Come again?" Wil says.

Gabe replies: "Goju is a fungus that performs exceptionally well in arid environments like that found here on Fury. I am surprised it is not more prevalent, to be honest."

"That light brown stuff? Looks like tofu?" Wil asks, remembering that there's a large container in one of the cupboards, left over from before Wil came aboard the *Ghos*—back when it was still the *Reaper*, under the command of Lanksham, the smuggler who saved him from dying alone in his damaged space-pod.

"I do not know what tofu is, but yes, goju is light brown. It can be prepared many ways and is a staple protein on less wealthy worlds."

"This way," Bennie says, turning left down a side street, following the map on his wristcomm. "Goju tastes like feet. If I never eat it again, it'll be too soon." He looks up at Wil. "You've probably eaten a ton of it, if you ever ate in a restaurant on this planet. It's everywhere."

"The things you learn," Wil says.

"Indeed," Gabe replies. Then the droid turns his head. "Captain, I believe we are being followed."

Wil turns his own head slightly, trying to look as if he's examining something in the shop window they're passing.

"Smooth," Bennie says, his voice dripping with sarcasm.

"Shut it," Wil mumbles, then takes a quick glance behind them. Without moving his mouth too much, he says, "I couldn't see anything."

"Four beings, approximately one hundred meters behind us."

"Wow, that's some distance," Wil says, then looks up at Gabe, a full head and a half taller than him. "Guess it wouldn't be that hard to keep tabs on us, bean pole."

Bennie cranes his neck. "Yeah, you kind stand out, Gabe."

Gabe is silent for a minute as they continue down the street, then says, "I believe I can remedy that." With some whirs and clicks, Gabe begins shrinking with each step, until he's the same height as Wil. "We should take a slight detour before our pursuers reacquire us in their sights." He takes a right down a narrow alley. Wil and Bennie hurry to keep up.

"Man, you're just full of all kind of tricks," Wil pants. "Those— what did you call them? Originals?—must have been all kinds of fun at parties back in super robot intelligence land."

Gabe studies his friend, "Nothing in the data I had access to indicated that the *Originals* engaged in partying. All indications point to them being a ruling class of cybernetic intelligence. I suspect they took their role quite seriously.

Bennie chuckles, but continues walking. "Come on, we're almost there."

"WHAT IS THAT PHRASE WIL USES? PENNY FOR YOUR THOUGHTS," Maxim says, sitting at the kitchenette table across from Zephyr, who's been sitting there silently for several centocks now, slowly spinning her glass of water.

"Has he ever said what a 'penny' is? They must be tremendously valuable, to be offered in exchange for one's thoughts," Zephyr replies. Maxim shakes his head: no. "I was thinking about what we talked about back on Brai. I mean, here we are working for Xarrix again, when it didn't end so well last time."

"To be fair, in a way, it did—end well, that is. I mean, we rescued Gabe, cleared our names, saved the Harrith system from being forced to join the GC, and exposed a massive conspiracy within the GC and Peacekeepers." The big man shrugs. "That's not nothing."

Zephyr nods. "You're right. On the larger scale, we did a tremendous amount of good. On the smaller scale, we nearly died —more than once—we were hunted by the Consortium for months, and we really didn't get paid all that well."

Maxim takes the glass from his companion, drinks the last of it, and gets up to put the empty glass in the cleaning unit. "I never thought I'd worry so much about money."

"Me either."

TEA, ANYONE?

"I believe this is our destination," Gabe says, as they walk up to what looks like a bar but has a sign outside showing that it is a teahouse.

Bennie points. "This? This is where Xarrix is operating out of?"

Wil shrugs. "Maybe he just likes tea? He didn't say this was one of his holdings, though I've never known him to meet anywhere he didn't own or at least control."

"He does, in fact, own this establishment," Gabe offers.

"How do you know?" Wil asks.

Gabe shrugs, "I hacked into the public records, which indicated a company called Gretix Holdings owned the building. Further research showed that Gretix Holdings is a subsidiary of Lothrop Incorporated, which, after more research, turns out is majority owned by Xarrix Cruthup. He leases the building to *Little Zady's Tea Emporium*, which he also owns."

Bennie looks up at Gabe. "Hey! The team already has a hacker." He glares at his metallic friend.

Wil chuckles. "Better watch out, man. Gabe might come for your job—ouch!" Wil sidesteps as a small fist strikes his groin. "Low blow," he wheezes.

Bennie grins and pushes through the doors of the tea shop.

Gabe looks at Wil. "I did not intend to insult Bennie. I am sure that if he had a wireless receiver within his body and the ability to control it without manual input, he could have accomplished the same thing." Gabe's new, more expressive face is much easier to read, and Wil can see he's genuinely worried that he's offended his friend.

Wil pats his shoulder. "Don't sweat it. I think Bennie is just annoyed with himself that he didn't think to do that research back on the *Ghost*, so when you did it just standing here," Wil shrugs, "he probably felt a little silly." He motions for Gabe to follow. "Come on, let's make sure he's not getting into trouble."

They enter the tea shop, and Wil is immediately surprised to find that it's an actual tea shop. *I kind of thought it'd be a bar*, he thinks, scanning the room. He spots two of Xarrix's goons standing near a booth, the privacy screen engaged. He motions to Bennie, who's standing near the bar, flirting with a Quillant bartender. *Does he ever stop?* Wil wonders.

"Hey, boys! You are boys, right? You know what, doesn't actually matter," Wil smiles as wide as he can. "Your boss in there?"

One goon looks Wil up and down, then looks at Bennie and Gabe, then reaches down and touches a control. The shimmering privacy screen dissolves, to reveal Xarrix sitting at a large booth, with Lorath and... "Cynthia!" Wil exclaims, sliding into the booth. "Guys, it's Cynthia, remember, from Harrith Prime, this past Garth-flak? She ruined it and tried to kill us."

"Yeah, I remember, she tried to kill me," Bennie grumbles, sliding in. Gabe, in his currently much smaller configuration, slides into the seat as well.

Cynthia, the feline-featured assistant to Lorath, grins at the small Brailack. "Sorry green stuff, Lorath only wanted your boss." She turns to Wil. "That little stunt caused quite a stir, you know?"

Once they are all in the booth, the privacy screen re-activates. Xarrix looks at Wil and the others. "That's all behind us. Clean slates and all that, yes?" He reaches over and pours two cups of tea, sliding one each over to Wil and Bennie. "Gabe, despite your new features, I assume you don't actually ingest food or drink?" He tilts his head and examines Gabe.

Gabe inclines his head in response. "You are correct, my new features are cosmetic only. My internal fusion core still generates the power I need to function."

Lorath makes what Wil assumes is a chuckle among her species.

"Yes, well." Xarrix turns back to Wil. "Let's get down to business, shall we?" he asks, spreading his arms expansively.

Wil nods. "Sure," he snaps his fingers. "Oh yeah, forgot. Gabe here is recording everything." He smiles and continues before Xarrix or Lorath can object, "Non-negotiable. You screwed me last time—your privacy screens always interfere with wristcomms—but Gabe has acquired special skills. After this, if you don't screw us, we won't need to record our conversations. But for now…" He trails off, still smiling.

"Fine," Xarrix grumbles, then continues, "I've been commissioned to help a certain individual salvage a derelict fleet—"

"A derelict fleet?" Bennie interrupts. He leans forward. "Who just leaves a fleet abandoned?"

Xarrix raises one hand and makes a pinching motion, cutting Bennie off. "As I was saying," he shoots a glare that would melt stone at Bennie, "this fleet is apparently a collection of rather massive cargo vessels. Old but still quite useful to my client."

"What type of vessels?" Gabe asks.

"I don't know and don't care," Xarrix replies. "The client wants these ships, she doesn't have the means to acquire them herself, and has hired me to facilitate." He spreads his hands. "I have hired several teams of salvagers but prefer to hedge my bets. The client isn't, how do you say? Trustworthy."

"Then why are you working with her?" Wil asks.

"Because her credits are good, of course." The Trenbal gangster smirks, taking a sip of his tea.

"So what? You want us as... muscle?" Wil pushes, "I mean we're not scrappers or salvagers."

"Score one for the human," Xarrix says, sliding his teacup away. "I need you, and one other group I've worked with before, to safeguard the expedition. The derelicts are in a more.... *wild* region of space. My understanding is that there could be some disgruntled ex-employees, and the like, in the area. Plus, having some additional muscle will help ensure that the client doesn't get any ideas."

Wil nods slowly. "Seems straightforward—"

Bennie starts choking on his tea. Gabe leans forward to look at his small friend as Wil continues, extending his hand. "I need to run the details by the others, but I think we're in."

Xarrix extends his own hand and shakes Wil's. "I still don't understand the significance of this," he says, tilting his head toward their two clasped hands.

"Let's just say it's a human thing." Wil lets go of Xarrix's hand and nudges Bennie, who is still trying to catch his breath, to exit the booth. "I'll be in touch."

"Don't take too long, the expedition departs in thirty tocks," Lorath offers, leering at Wil as he slides out of the booth.

"Was great to see you too, Lorath. And you Cynthia, always an absolute pleasure." Wil smiles and shoves Bennie to hop out of the booth. With a wave he leads his crew away from the booth, the privacy screen re-activating behind them. He turns to Bennie. "What the hell's wrong with you?"

Bennie looks up. "Sorry, must be allergic or something."

"So weird. Alright, thoughts?"

"I assume you are asking about working for Xarrix, not Bennie's allergies?" Gabe offers.

Wil nods. "Yeah. He's a dick of the highest order, no doubt. But money up front, and sounds like a ton of it—that's enticing."

"I concur," Gabe says, as they turn a corner heading back towards the spaceport. "But I suggest, should we take this opportunity, that we be extremely vigilant."

TOO MANY CRIMES TO REMEMBER

"Ah crap," Bennie mutters.

Gabe and Wil both look up the street at the half-dozen aliens of as many different species waiting there, all in dark red robs, hoods up over their heads. "Who're these guys?" Wil asks. The only difference between these six and every other robed alien nearby is that the six approaching have dark gray sashes with some type of badge on it across their bodies.

"I believe four of them are the same beings who were following us previously," Gabe says.

"Great," Wil mutters. "We haven't broken any of their laws or whatever." He looks down at Bennie. "Have we?"

Bennie shrugs. "No. I mean, I don't think so."

"You do not think so?" Gabe asks. The group of robed aliens has changed course and is following them towards the alleyway that leads back to the spaceport. Gabe stops. "Captain, this alley does not have an exit."

Wil sighs and stops dead in his tracks. He turns back toward their pursuers. "Hi there, fellas. Is there something we can do for you?"

The leader of the group steps forward, reaching up to lower his hood, revealing Quillant features. He points to Bennie. "Ben-Ari Vulvo, you must come with us, by order of the high clergy of Ulop."

"I knew it," Wil mutters, looking down at Bennie. "Can't take you anywhere!" he hisses. Looking back up at the Quillant and his friends, he adds, "Listen, fellas, we're not sure who this Ben array vulva is, but," gesturing to Bennie, "this isn't him. This is my valet, Alfred."

Bennie bows, but says nothing.

The Quillant smiles. "A DNA scan can clear this up easily. Please, travelers, come with us." The Quillant turns, gesturing back towards the alley's only exit. His compatriots step back, creating an opening. "Please."

"What exactly did this Ben-Ari character do?" Gabe asks, not taking a step.

"Ben-Ari Vulvo is accused of hacking into the church's mainframe and stealing highly sensitive information." The leader glares at Bennie.

"They weren't paying their taxes," Bennie starts, then clamps his mouth shut.

"Sweet boneless nudon, dude!" Wil says, pushing his long brown coat aside to quickly draw his pulse pistol, shooting at the building over the heads of the crowd of now angry robed aliens. "Everyone on the ground!" Wil shouts. Beside him, he hears a whirring sound from Gabe and glances over. One of Gabe's hands has transformed into a large blaster. "That's new," Wil says.

Gabe nods. "I have been experimenting with my body's ability to reconfigure some of its components. A side effect, as it were, of being designed by the Amalgamation of Parts. What do you think?" He raises his gun-arm and tilts it from side to side.

Before Wil can answer a shot rings out and an energy blast strikes Gabe in the chest, narrowly missing Wil's head. Without missing a beat, Gabe lowers his arm and fires at the offending zealot, dropping the being to the ground. "Stunned," Gabe offers, moving toward the others, all now lying prone on the ground.

"You cannot escape Ben-Ari!" the lead zealot says, looking up from the ground. He starts to rise, then jitters slightly and collapses, a wave of energy washing over him. Wil glances at Gabe, just as his blaster arm is reconfiguring back into his hand.

"Let's go already!" Bennie says in a loud whisper, as they exit the alley and jog towards the spaceport. Gabe reaches down and picks the little hacker up, tucking him under his arm.

"Bennie, I hate you sometimes," Wil says. "What did you steal?"

"Gods, I don't even remember!" the little hacker shouts as he bounces under Gabe's arm. "I was hired by, who was it? Oh, that's right. Some syndicate guys hired me, I think from Odolar, to dig up the data the church guys were hiding."

"What was it?" Gabe asks, glancing down. They've slowed their pace after taking several turns. "The data, I mean. You mentioned that the church was not paying their taxes."

"Beyond that, no idea," Bennie says, as Gabe lowers him to the ground.

"You expect us to believe you didn't look?" Wil asks. "You've gone through everyone's quarters and rummaged through their stuff. Of course you looked."

"Oh, I definitely looked, it just wasn't interesting. I got to the tax stuff and started to zone out. I sent the file to the client, archived my copy and went to dinner, if I recall correctly." He looks up at Wil and smirks. "Also, I only go through your stuff."

"Why you little!" Wil makes a grab for the little Brailack, who expertly dodges and trots on ahead a few steps. "Hate him," Wil mutters again.

THAT'S A LOT OF MONEY

Back aboard the *Ghost*, now siting in orbit over Fury and safely out of reach of the religious zealots that run Pulto City, Wil leans back against the lounge sofa. "So, we all good with this?" He looks around. Zephyr and Maxim are sitting together at the small kitchenette table. Gabe is standing near the hatch leading towards engineering and Bennie is sitting in a chair facing the sofa.

Bennie raises his hand. "I say we do it. It sounds straightforward, and the money is good—correction, the money is *great*."

"Nothing is ever straightforward where Xarrix is concerned," Zephyr offers, looking at Bennie. "You should know that."

"Well, sure," Bennie replies. "But the money is outstanding."

"While I have no strong opinion one way or the other, I will say that our current financial situation is at least not so dire as to make taking this opportunity a must," Gabe offers. "However, Bennie is correct in his assessment of the sum."

Wil nods once. "Gabe's right. Money-wise we can pass on this job and be okay. Bennie's folks paid a hefty reward for rescuing Len-Lu." He looks at Bennie. "Maybe someone will kidnap her again?" Bennie sticks his tongue out in reply.

"You mean, Bee-Bees parents?" Maxim asks, not even a hint of a smile on his face.

Bennie raises both fists and slams them together as he raises his arms, then for good measure sticks his tongue out again.

Wil just stares for a moment. "What—the hell—was that?"

"*Friends*." Bennie says, smiling. "Ross Geller, I like him."

Wil chuckles. "I was always partial to Chandler. Anyway, sounds like there aren't any strong nays, am I wrong there?" He looks around the room at each member of his crew in turn. Each shakes their head. "Okay then." He tilts his head upward. "Computer, open a channel to Xarrix."

"Working," the ship replies.

After a moment, the telltale soft beep announces that they're connected. "You've made a decision?" the crime lord asks.

"We have. We'll take the job. You know the deal, pay upfront."

"That's excellent news. My representative will bring the payment on a transfer stick when they come aboard."

"I'm sorry, what now? Who's coming aboard? For what reason?" Wil asks, glancing at Maxim and Zephyr who have visibly tensed.

"You didn't expect me to pay you all that money upfront with no way to ensure you didn't go back on your word—"

"You son of a—" Wil starts.

Xarrix makes a hissing sound, silencing Wil. "Do not forget, it was you who broke the deal between us first, by trying to keep the droid."

"His name is—" Wil starts, again.

"I don't care," Xarrix continues, cutting over Wil. "My representative will be aboard your ship for the duration of the operation, to ensure you do not cross me." He pauses, then adds, with a smile in his voice, "Look at this way, you get the payment without worrying about transfer intercepts, and you get to make a new friend. I know how much you were dying for friends not so long ago. You'll receive the coordinates shortly." Before anyone can say anything else, the soft beep of the comm system lets them know Xarrix has terminated the call.

"Asshole," Maxim mutters, then looks at Wil. "I used that right, right?"

"Most definitely, buddy." Wil looks around. "Okay, let's hang here and prep the ship for our visitor. Bennie and Zee, go get one of the guest berths ready. Maxim, run a diagnostic on the weapons systems—let's make sure we're solid there." He looks at Gabe. "Everything good down in Gabe town?"

Gabe tilts his head. "By Gabe town you mean engineering? Yes, everything is operational and within acceptable tolerance ranges. We are, as you say, good to go." He smiles, then turns serious. "Captain, we should be cautious on this mission. It is one thing to work with Xarrix again, but to have one of his operatives aboard poses a significant risk to the ship and crew."

Wil places a hand on the shiny metallic shoulder. "No argument there my friend. We'll be careful."

"Can you configure the terminal to capture everything that goes on in here?" Zephyr asks Bennie, as they enter the guest berth to be assigned to Xarrix's representative. "I suspect knowing what goes on in here may be of value at some point."

Bennie gives the Palorian woman a sly look. "Sure I can. You're not worried that's a little, you know, invasive?"

Zephyr shakes her head. "Whomever this person is, they are not our friend or even our ally. They're here to make sure we do the job Xarrix has paid for and to spy on us." She looks around the room. "They will likely try to kill us at the first reasonable opportunity."

Bennie shudders. "You think it's Lorath?" he asks, taking a seat at the terminal built into the small desk in the corner of the room. "I mean, who else would he trust to watch over us?"

"Could be. She *is* Xarrix's right hand. It would make sense to put her with the crew he trusts the least." Zephyr moves to the small dresser and opens each drawer, making sure the previous occupant has not left anything behind. She picks up a small bundle of data cards. "I suppose it depends on who the other crew he's hired as protection is."

Over the ship's address system, Wil's voice announces, "We're about to dock with Xarrix's ship. Maxim and Zephyr, meet me at the port airlock."

Zephyr glances at Bennie. "Looks like we're about to find out the answer to that. Hurry up in here," she adds, as she stalks out of the room.

"Any communication with the ship?" Zephyr asks, joining Maxim and Wil outside the airlock.

Wil shakes his head. "Nope—just got the coordinates, then this shuttle arrived." He looks at his wristcomm. "They're docked." He reaches over to the control panel and presses a button, opening the outer doors.

A single space-suited figure walks in and presses a control on the inside of the airlock, closing the outer doors. Wil presses another control and after a brief moment allowing the airlock to fill with a breathable atmosphere, the inner doors open. "Welcome aboard the *Ghost*," Wil says as the figure steps into the ship, dropping a duffel bag to the ground.

The new arrival reaches up and twists the helmet, releasing the seals, then lifts it up off its head. "Thank you, Captain. It's a pleasure to be aboard."

"Cynthia," Zephyr growls.

CHAPTER IX

WERDLOW? NEVER HEARD OF IT

Cynthia walks over and hands her helmet to Zephyr. "Long time no see," she purrs as she walks by. Zephyr only growls again.

"Oh, this should be fun," Maxim says, turning to watch her leave, then exhaling loudly as Zephyr thrusts a spacesuit helmet into his midsection. Zephyr storms after the feline-featured criminal.

"What could go wrong?" Wil asks, turning to follow the two women, patting Maxim on the arm as he passes him.

Entering the lounge, Wil finds Cynthia sliding her spacesuit off and handing it to Zephyr, who promptly tosses it onto the couch. "Okay, so we're stuck with you, but there are ground rules, cat-ninja-assistant-crime-boss-lady." Wil levels a finger at Cynthia.

"I'm Tygran, have you really never met another of my people?" She smirks and drops into a chair, where she drapes one leg over an arm, her tail swishing lazily.

Wil shakes his head once, then continues, "You're a guest aboard this ship, so you can come and go as you like in the lounge and crew berth section. If you shed, you clean it up. Once we get where we're going, you're welcome on the bridge, but not before. Engineering and the cargo hold are off limits." He gestures to the kitchenette in one corner of the room. "We tend to eat meals together. You can join, or not."

"Sounds fine to me. Anything else?"

"Yes," Zephyr answers. "How did you survive that firefight on Harrith? Or get away from the authorities?"

"Or that crime boss, what's his name?" Wil adds.

"Hoob," Cynthia offers.

"Yeah, him," Zephyr says.

"It might surprise you how far Xarrix and Lorath's reach goes, even on Harrith. That Hoob character was a handful, I admit. I lost some good men fighting him and his goons off. When the planetary security service showed up, he crawled back under whatever rock he came from before they secured the area. We sat in detention for a day, no big deal." She shrugs, smiling. "Overall, it wasn't too bad." She arches her back, stretching, "The bed wasn't very comfortable though."

Just then Bennie walks in from the crew berth area. "Cynthia?"

"Hi, pipsqueak," she waves.

Bennie gestures to the lounging woman. "This is who we have to keep with us?"

"Afraid so," Zephyr says, grabbing the discarded spacesuit and heading back toward the airlock and armory. "I'll grab her bag."

"Great." Bennie gestures back toward the hatch he just came through. "Your room is that way."

Cynthia starts to get up before Wil says, "Not so fast. There's the little matter of payment, and then details. Xarrix said you'd have both." He gestures over to the terminal set into the bulkhead near the kitchenette.

Cynthia reaches inside a pocket of her tight-fitting jumpsuit, and retrieves a small device no more significant than her thumb. She tosses it to Wil, who throws it to Bennie. "Check it." Bennie nods and heads to the terminal. "Okay, while he does that, details. What're we doing?"

Cynthia sits up in the chair and looks right at Wil. "Holoprojector?" Wil gestures to a console set in the coffee table next to her. She retrieves another data stick and inserts it into a slot on the table console. The surface of the table comes to life, showing a section of the galaxy Wil isn't familiar with, just as Zephyr walks in with Maxim and takes a seat on the couch next to him.

"This is just outside the Neglool sector," Cynthia says. The image rotates and zooms to show several blue dots—dozens, in fact. "These are our targets. They're all adrift in a relatively tight formation, here." She gestures to the dots. "This is twelve light-years from Werdlow Three, which is where our client is."

"Werdlow?" Zephyr asks. "That system is classified as badlands." She looks at Wil. "The Peacekeepers gave up trying to 'civilize' the system and its neighbors several tens of cycles ago. The last I heard, Werdlow Three was home to some low-rent warlord who'd taken control of the system."

"Be careful not to use that term if you meet our client," Cynthia smiles. "She prefers the term 'Duchess,' since warlord sounds so malevolent and masculine." She chuckles. "And *low rent* just sounds insulting. Warlord suits her just fine, as she's one of the cruelest beings I've ever met." Cynthia shakes her head slightly. "I'm getting off track. These—" and she gestures to the blue dots, "—are some type of massive ships, freighters of some kind, we assume. She wants them to create a maritime fleet to begin building her empire so that she can expand beyond Werdlow. She sees shipping as the key."

"You said she's a warlord. What's she need with empire building at this point?" Wil asks, leaning forward, staring at the hovering blue dots.

"Werdlow is a relatively poor system, so are its neighbors. That's why it was so easy for the Peacekeepers to designate the region badlands and be done," Cynthia replies. "With a fleet of ships, she'll be able to create a shipping empire overnight."

"So, evil space UPS? Got it." Wil says.

OFF WE GO

"Dropping from FTL in a few minutes," Will announced. He looks over at Cynthia, who is sitting at one of the unused bridge stations. "You sure we'll be welcome?"

The feline-featured criminal nods slowly. "Xarrix and Lorath are already here, so are the other security contractor and the client. You'll be fine."

Maxim looks up from his console. "Since we're almost there, why don't you tell us about this other group that Xarrix has hired?"

Cynthia smiles at the large ex-Peacekeeper. "I don't know who they are. Xarrix hired them and never told me who it was. I don't even know if Lorath knew who they were before they arrived."

"Sure are a lot of unknowns," Bennie says, from his station.

"Agreed," Gabe says.

"And that's why you're being paid so well," the Tygran woman replies, then points to the main display. "Oh look, we're there."

Wil grumbles something under his breath, then focuses on the ship's controls. Reaching over, he pulls back the FTL slide and the main screen changes from long, stretched-out rainbow lines to regular everyday pinpricks of light.

"I heard that, and wouldn't you like to know?" the Tygran

chuckles, then turns to her station. "I'm contacting Xarrix and Lorath now."

The screen changes, and Xarrix is looking at the crew from the bridge of a ship Wil doesn't recognize. He smiles. "Kinda weird to not see you sitting in a booth at a bar."

Xarrix laughs, which sounds like a rasping cough, then stops. "Always with the jokes. I wonder how funny you'd find it if I dropped a viral bomb on your mudball planet? I'm certain I could get in and out of your home star system without a Peacekeeper patrol ever noticing." His eyes narrow as he leans forward and stares directly at Wil. "Would that be funny?"

Wil chokes on whatever he was about to say and just asks, "Are we ready to go?"

Xarrix smirks. "Almost. Come aboard the *Berserker*. Duchess Jurrella wants to meet the entire command staff for this little endeavor."

Maxim looks up from his station. "Not a very apt name." He gestures to one of the smaller sub-screens near the front of the bridge, which is showing a long-range view of what could at best be called a battleship class vessel. Ancient and very under-maintained, but still enormous. Several of its gun emplacements are barren, and there are meters-wide patches across its hull.

On the main screen Xarrix clears his throat. "Just you. Your crew can remain aboard the *Ghost*."

"No deal, man," Wil says, but Xarrix interrupts.

"It is not negotiable. Cynthia, ensure he does as he's told." The screen goes back to showing the section of space in front of the *Ghost*, which now includes the rapidly approaching battleship.

Zephyr turns to Cynthia. "Excuse me, what? Ensure he does as he's told? And how exactly will you be doing that?" Her hand is resting on the pulse pistol she wears in a hip holster.

Cynthia waves one hand. "Calm down, everyone." She turns to Wil, "Don't start this little outing on the wrong foot." She gets up and leaves the bridge.

"I dislike her," Gabe offers.

"You and me both, buddy," Wil says, working the controls, bringing the *Ghost* closer to the *Berserker*. "Zephyr, can you take the controls? I may have to go alone, but I don't have to go unprepared." He stands up and heads toward the bridge hatch. Gabe follows.

As Wil and Gabe enter the armory, below the bridge, Gabe says, "Captain, I do not have a good feeling about this. I would like to amend my earlier statements regarding my acceptance of this project."

"No takebacks, pal," Wil says, grabbing his modular armor. *Probably be rude to show up in that Harrith power armor of mine*, he thinks, attaching the armored cuff around his wristcomm.

"Is that a concept on your planet? Taking back things that have already been said?" Gabe asks, reaching up on a high shelf and grabbing a slim combat pack that Wil can wear under his duster without it showing.

Wil takes the pack and slips it on. "Thanks. No, well, sorta. The no take-backs thing is a phrase as old as Earth, I'm sure. It's just my people's way of accepting that what's in the past, is past. You can't take back your approval any more than I could not set a course for the rendezvous point where we picked up Cynthia." Wil shrugs. "All we can do now is make the best of the situation as it evolves." He slides an armor plate onto his chest, the powerful magnets locking into to concealed attachment points in the under-layer he always wears under his every-day jumpsuit. Wil grabs his brown leather duster and says, "Okay, let's get this party started."

MEET THE TEAM

As Wil exits the armory, a metallic hand rests on his shoulder. "Take this," Gabe offers, holding out a small device with a blinking blue light. It's no longer than Wil's thumb and twice as wide.

"What is it?" he asks, turning it over, before shoving it in a shoulder pocket of his jumpsuit. There's a soft thud against the hull, and Zephyr announces over the comms, "We're docked. They say we have to clear out to make room for the other ship."

"A precaution," Gabe says, walking over and opening the inner doors of the airlock.

Cynthia turns the corner. "Precaution?"

Walking into the airlock, Wil nods. "Thanks, pal. Never you mind," he says to Cynthia. Wil smiles at Gabe as the door closes on them both, then reaches over and presses the control to open the outer doors. The indicator shows a solid seal and atmosphere on the other side. The outer doors slide open to reveal a telescoping boarding tube connecting the *Ghost* to the *Berserker*. He looks over at Cynthia. "Come on, pussycat."

It takes only a moment for the two to drift from one ship to the other, the outer airlock doors opening as they arrive. Once inside the airlock, the exterior doors begin to close and the docking tube retracts. On the other side of the inner doors, Wil can see Lorath waiting for them. Wil glances over at Cynthia. "Oh look, your boss."

"Welcome aboard the *Berserker*, the lounge is right this way," Lorath says, turning and heading off down the corridor without looking to see if Wil is following.

Looking around himself, Wil comments, "So, Lorath old pal. Who's this other group Xarrix is hiring as security?"

The scales along the back of Lorath's neck shift: pink then purple, then a reddish color, then back. She doesn't turn her head. "They're docking as soon as your ship vacates. You'll meet their captain soon enough."

"Awesome, surprises," Wil says, as they enter the central lounge. As lounges go, it's somewhere better than the one on the *Ghost* but not quite as opulent as the one on Bennie's parents' yacht. Wil lets out a low whistle, taking in the scene. Xarrix is sitting near the back of the room, next to a raised dais with what might charitably be called a throne.

On it sits a woman, judging by the sari-like outfit she's wearing. An elaborate headscarf is wrapped around the top of her head. He skin is a jet black, with bright blue freckles. Her yellow pupil-less eyes seem to take in the entire room. The rest of the room is filled by several long tables with assorted alien species sitting at them, talking amongst themselves.

Seeing Wil enter, Xarrix motions to him. "Wil Calder! Come over here!" The reptilian gangster seems happier than he had been a little while ago.

Lorath and Cynthia peel off from Wil as he heads towards the throne, finding something to discuss that isn't near the female warlord.

"Wil Calder, Captain of the *Ghost*. I have the pleasure of introducing you to the Duchess Jurrella of the planet Werdlow Three," Xarrix says, pulling Wil closer to the throne.

Wil bows slightly. "It's a pleasure to meet you—uh, Duchess."

He looks up at her smiling face. The smile doesn't reach her eyes, and Wil notices that her each of her teeth seem to be filed to a point. It doesn't look natural. "Lovely ship you have here," he gulps, trying to back away, but is stopped by Xarrix.

Jurrella eyes Wil. "I like this one. Though he seems rather puny and frail." Her teeth make her words rasp slightly. Wil notices that instead of a nose, she has two large slits that flex as she inhales.

Wil straightens. "Woah, woah—"

Xarrix interrupts. "Wil has worked with me before—he's an accomplished pilot and smuggler. I am sure you heard about the 'Harrith Incident'? That was Captain Calder and his crew."

Jurrella nods. "I'm familiar with the exploits of the crew of the *Ghost.*" She claps her hands together. "Quite an exciting life you lead, young Captain."

Wil glances at Xarrix, then back to Jurrella. "Uh, thanks."

"Xarrix Cruthup!" a voice booms from the opposite side of the room, from the corridor that leads to the airlock.

As Wil and Xarrix turn, Wil hears Xarrix groan, then force a jovial tone. "Follux Sul! Welcome!"

Wil turns to see what he can only describe as a leprechaun—not the cereal box kind, but the horror movie kind. Oh, and it also has a mechanical leg and arm. "The hell is that thing?" Wil asks under his breath.

Xarrix murmurs, "Buttoxian." He walks towards the diminutive starship Captain. "Follux Sul, it's been too long." Xarrix places a fist across his chest.

The Buttoxian reaches up and matches the gesture, his mechanical arm making small hissing noises as it moves. "Indeed it has, you old scoundrel. I see you haven't driven Lorath off." He turns and nods to the imposing henchwoman, who nods back. "No idea why she stays with you," he smiles a gilded and jeweled smile. Any teeth not encrusted in jewels or covered in gold are yellow.

Xarrix shrugs, "I pay well, and let her do as she likes. Come, meet our host."

AWKWARD DINNER PARTIES

"Now that everyone is here, introductions are in order!" Jurrella announces, walking down the steps of her throne. She gestures to Xarrix. "Please do the honors."

Xarrix nods and clears his throat. Wil notices that the rest of the room must be hangers-on of Jurrella's and ship's crew. "Yes, thank you Duchess, our esteemed client, and ruler of Werdlow Three." He gestures to Follux Sul. "Follux Sul and his crew have worked for me many times, doing some of the more unsavory work that is often required in my line of work. He's a consummate professional and will keep our salvage teams safe. My number two, Lorath, will work aboard his vessel as a liaison." He nods to Follux Sul, who nods back, smiling widely.

"Wil Calder is a human," Xarrix says. He pauses as Jurrella and many others start to murmur. "His world is not part of the GC. He and his crew are responsible for stopping the Peacekeepers from invading the Harrith sector." More murmuring and head nodding. Wil is blushing. "You may have heard about the incident out near the edge of the GC at Borrolo—that was them too. He and his crew are very dedicated and will make sure no harm comes to the salvagers." He smiles his reptilian smile at Wil. "They're excellent at not dying."

The introductions continue. Many around the table are in fact the salvage teams who will man the small tug freighters that will board the derelicts. They're a mishmash of races, including many Wil has never encountered. After that, Jurrella tells everyone to take a seat for a feast to mark the beginning of the endeavor that will transform her system into one the GC wants to interact with.

Wil ends up sitting across the table from Follux Sul and next to Lorath. He leans over to Xarrix's second. "So, you get to ride herd on the munchkin and his crew. Was there like a paper-rock-scissors kind of thing? Winner gets the *Ghost*?" He smiles.

"In fact, I chose to supervise Follux Sul. Believe it or not, babysitting you and your band of losers is the easy job," she sneers as she pushes a scoop of something Wil hasn't been able to identify around her plate with a piece of bread. She takes a bite, never letting her eyes off Wil. When she finishes chewing, she adds, "His team is the one Xarrix hires for the jobs he doesn't think you can do."

"What's that mean?" Wil asks, looking at something on his plate that is wriggling away from his fork. "What jobs does Xarrix have that I couldn't or wouldn't do? I've smuggled weapons and supplies, stolen merchandise…" He looks at her, without blinking. "…robbed super secret space stations owned by the Consortium."

Lorath looks Wil in the eye, then begins to tick things off on her clawed fingers. "Transporting slaves. Destroying food shipments for non-payment. Hijacking. The occasional murder or assassination… once he asked Follux Sul to de-orbit a small orbital habitat." Wil is staring, his mouth hanging open. "You're going to attract flies like that," she says, then turns to the grinning Follux Sul, sitting across the table. "How have you been, Follux?"

The evil leprechaun pirate smiles his jewel-encrusted smile at her. "Quite well. We recently came to run a small piracy operation near Bentux."

"Oh?" Lorath says.

"Killing the leader and his lieutenants helped encourage the rest of the gang to fall in line behind me and mine. Very lucrative. I'm surprised Xarrix didn't tell you about it, as he's the one who provided the location of their base, and some special weapons for the task." He glances at Wil, who is listening, while trying to make it look like his food has been eaten without actually taking a bite. "Apparently, they were behind on payments for some rather nasty weapons Xarrix had sold them."

"Harsh," Wil mutters.

Follux Sul looks from Lorath to Wil. "What about you, Wil Calder? You seem a bit honorable to be among this group, what with saving the galaxy and all. How'd you end up working with Xarrix?"

Wil smiles while chewing on something he can't identify, trying to think of a reply. To buy more time, he takes a sip of the grum in front of him. "Well, it doesn't pay as well as you might think, saving the galaxy. Though the *Ghost* got a complete overhaul from the Ankarrans all on the Harrithian's dime, so that was nice. I've been working with Xarrix since I got the *Ghost* actually. He hooked me up with work and even helped me find my crew. Backstabbing crime-boss notwithstanding, he's done me some solids." Wil shrugs. "This job sounded interesting."

Follux grins. "That's right! You came aboard in that Ankarran Raptor. Very nice ship, for an older model, that is."

Wil glowers, turning to look the diminutive pirate in the eye. "Excuse me."

The Buttoxian pirate spreads his hands wide. "The Ankarran Raptor, model 89, was a great ship in its time. I know many a pirate who tried to get their hands on one when they came out. Alas, as usual, the Peacekeepers kept most of them for themselves." He grins. "The model 92, now that's a fighting machine."

"I'll have to see if I can find one and get a tour," Wil says, taking a sip of his drink.

"I'd be happy to show you around. My ship, the *Butcher*, is a model 92." Follux's smile, while enormous, is not at all friendly and doesn't reach his eyes.

Wil nearly chokes on his drink. "You have a Raptor? I didn't think there were that many, outside Ankarra or Peacekeeper special forces." Wil looks at Lorath, who just shrugs and turns to talk to a being that looks to Wil like a Teenage Mutant Ninja Turtle—only orange, its shell covered in spikes, and with three eyes.

"Oh yes, my friend, they are quite rare. I understand you stumbled onto yours? Quite impressive, that. I got the *Butcher* the old-fashioned way—I killed her Captain and crew while they were aboard a space station getting drunk. Once her crew was dead and her own fate sealed, getting the command codes from the Captain was easy. Her threshold for pain was surprisingly low."

Wil stares down the little pirate. "First of all, I didn't stumble onto the *Ghost*. She was given to me when her Captain and crew—people I genuinely liked, mostly—were murdered in cold blood by some Hulgian assholes and a Peacekeeper scumbag named Janus. Second," Wil pauses, "Fuck you." He gets up and heads towards the back of the lounge. Looking over at Xarrix, he calls, "Been fun. I'll be on my ship, holler when we're ready to get underway." Without waiting for an answer, he exits the room, lifting his wristcomm to his mouth. "Come get me."

PART THREE

CHAPTER X

THAT'S A LOT OF SHIPS

The party aboard the *Berserker* goes on for what feels like forever to the crew of the *Ghost*. Eventually, the *Butcher* docks with the massive battleship, picking up its captain, and the order is given to get underway.

Follux Sul wasn't lying about his ship: it looks like the *Ghost* in the most superficial of ways, but her engines are more significant, and her forward weapons—both those on the engine nacelles and above and behind the bridge—are much fiercer looking. Add to that a much sleeker overall appearance, and the *Butcher* looks like a much meaner vessel than the *Ghost*.

As Wil brings the ship out of FTL, Bennie complains, "It didn't look that far on the holo-map."

"Maybe it wasn't to scale," Wil says, looking over the tactical map showing on the main screen at the front of the bridge. "Wow, that's a lot of ships. Right?" He looks at Cynthia, who's taken up residence at an unused bridge station directly behind Wil's command and pilot station. She just shrugs and goes back to filing one of her claws, with a large metal file Wil is sure came from engineering.

Zephyr nods. "More than Xarrix mentioned, that's for sure." She looks down at her console. "Incoming comm. It's Xarrix."

She taps a control and Xarrix's voice enters the bridge. "I'm transmitting your assignment now. It'll include the ships you are to protect and patrol routes you're to fly. Your primary objective is ensuring that the salvage teams can come and go between the derelicts, safely."

"How hot is this area?" Wil asks. "I didn't even know there was anything here, how could anyone else? Excluding Jurrella, of course. Far as I can tell, we're light years from the nearest trade route or system."

Xarrix smiles tightly. "Our client's organization isn't as airtight as, say, my own. She believes word may have gotten out." He looks past Wil to Cynthia. "Make sure our best interests are looked after."

The Tygran looks up, making a purring noise. "Of course."

The screen goes black, then switches back to the tactical overview of the region of space the *Ghost* is in. Wil presses a control, changing the view to the forward sensors. The display now shows at least a hundred ships drifting at odd angles to one another. Weirder still... "They're all nearly identical," Wil comments to no one in particular.

"You're right," Maxim confirms from his station, looking down at his tactical scanners. "They're not all the same size or mass, but design-wise they're nearly identical." He looks over at Zephyr. "Have you ever seen a ship like this?"

His companion consults her own displays briefly before answering, shaking her head. "No, nothing like these are in the database, at least not that I could find. They're so beautiful." She looks at the main display, where the massive, green flattened-egg shapes are floating on screen.

Each ship is at least half a kilometer long, with many coming in at nearly two. There aren't any discernible engines to indicate which is the front of back of the vessel.

Cynthia clears her throat. "Very pretty, yes. We should get going, look—" she gestures to the lower corner of the main display, where the salvager ships they've been assigned to protect are on the move. "Don't want to fail in the first tock of your assignment, right?" she grins. Standing up, she adds, "I'll be in the lounge."

The mix of freighters and tugs moves as a unit towards what Wil assumes is a randomly selected ship. The tugs begin using bucking cables to pull themselves against the giant ship's hulls.

"I really don't like her," Zephyr growls.

"I don't know, I'm warming up to her," Bennie says, hopping out of his chair. "I'll be in the lounge."

Maxim makes a face. "Explains why there are so many Brailack in the galaxy."

Wil and Zephyr both laugh, then Wil turns his attention to the main display and his flight controls. "I'll keep us a hundred or so kilometers from the derelict, per Xarrix's instructions. Zephyr, can you reach out and let them know?"

"Roger that. I wonder why he doesn't want us to get too close to the ships?" she asks.

"I wonder the same," Wil says. "By the way, Max, keep an eye on the *Butcher*. I don't trust that little Lucky Charms motherfucker as far as I can throw him."

"Lucky Charms?" Maxim asks, then shakes his head. "Never mind, and I concur. I read up on Follux Sul—or at least as much as possible, as his public record is pretty light. Before we departed, I reached out to a friend in the Peacekeepers, and since I'm no longer a felon and traitor, he did me a favor and sent over Sul's Peace-keeper file, which is *considerably* more detailed."

Wil turns to his big friend. "And when exactly were you going to mention this to me?"

Maxim shrugs. "Now?"

Wil tuts. "Hmmmm, what've you got?"

Zephyr crosses to the bridge hatch, where she presses a control on the panel next to it. The panel turns red, she looks at Wil. "Just in case our cat-ninja comes back."

Maxim works his console, bringing up a Peacekeeper file on the main display. In the top right corner is a picture of Follux Sul. "Lorath wasn't exaggerating when she told you what he's been up to. He's wanted on seven worlds the Peacekeepers have contracts with, for offenses ranging from extortion to attempted genocide." He scrolls the file on the display up. "He's also wanted in several of the unincorporated areas, particularly Flad Denor, for 'crimes against the people,' whatever that means."

"Damn," Wil says, reading as the file continues to scroll. "This is one seriously evil leprechaun."

Maxim and Zephyr exchange a look, then both shrug.

BENNIE PLOPS DOWN ON THE SOFA NEXT TO CYNTHIA. "SO, LOOKS like we'll be sitting around with time to kill. What do your people like to do for fun?" If Brailack had eyebrows, his would be waggling —but since they don't, just his green eyelids bounce up and down.

The feline-featured assistant criminal leers at Bennie. "I don't think you could handle what I like for fun."

Resting his small green hand on her light brown furred hand, he murmurs, "Why don't we find out?"

SPAGHETTI FACTORY

"So, they'll start tomorrow?" Maxim asks, sitting at the kitchenette table. Everyone, including Cynthia, is present.

Zephyr nods. "Yes, according to the Captain of the *Huflo* their initial inspection shows several places they think they can dock and cut through the hull. The *Plo* has most of their equipment, so they want to make sure it can dock."

Wil looks over at Cynthia. "Have you heard from Lorath about the other team? They have anything yet?"

Taking her fork and spinning it, she looks down at the mass of noodles on her plate. Lifting the fork, she eyes the mass. "About the same. The *Erabi* is the lead ship of their salvager group. They scanned one of the smaller vessels, found a few places they think they can cut in." She leans down and takes a bite of her spaghetti, biting off the noodles that linger on the fork, letting them drop to the plate, red sauce staining the fur on her chin. "Needs meat," she says, licking her lips and sizable incisors.

Maxim leans in, helping himself to a second helping. "This is quite good. Not as good as tacos, but a close second."

"Go easy on the parm, that's the last tube," Wil says, pointing to the tall green cylinder of 'one hundred percent grated parmesan cheese' in Maxim's hand.

"It's quite good, you should have gotten more when you went home." The big Palorian sets the container back on the table.

"I didn't know I'd be feeding so many," Wil says, scooping up a bit more of the noodles and rich red sauce.

Cynthia watches all this. "How long has it been since you went back to your home world?"

Wil sets his fork down. "Hmm. I guess it's been four years now, give or take. Why?"

"Just wondering. That's a long time to be away from home."

"He doesn't have a choice," Zephyr growls, then takes a bite of spaghetti as Maxim rests a hand on her leg under the table. At his touch, some of her tension drains away.

"Oh? I knew you were the only one, Xarrix mentioned your people being pretty primitive. If that's the case, how are you here, flying this ship? Surely the Peacekeepers are still patrolling primitive, pre-contact systems?" She looks at Zephyr, who nods.

Wil smiles sadly. "Long story, maybe I'll tell it to you one day." He cocks an eyebrow at her. "You know, when you're not a sort of evil overseer watching my every move."

Cynthia purrs, loud enough for everyone at the table to hear, then raises her glass in a toast, smiling, her lip stuck on her incisor.

From across the table, Zephyr growls again. "I'm not hungry." She gets up and storms out of the lounge. Maxim looks at her retreating back, then at Wil and Cynthia, then back to where the hatch to the crew quarters is closing behind Zephyr . He gets up and follows.

Bennie reaches across the table for Maxim's plate. "More for the rest of us," he says, dumping the contents of Maxim's plate on to his. "He's right, you really should have gotten more of this parma-gram cheese."

"Parmesan," Wil corrects, then looks at Cynthia. "So how does someone like you get stuck working for someone like Xarrix?"

She grins. "Someone like me? Like me how?"

Wil blushes slightly. "I mean, you seem intelligent—"

"And hot," Bennie interrupts. "Ouch!" He jerks as if struck, then glares at Wil.

"Don't you have some place to be?" Wil asks, looking at Gabe, who's been standing silently, as usual, off to the side of the dining area.

Taking the hint, Gabe says, "Indeed, we have a series a of diagnostics to run on the main computer."

"No, we don't," Bennie says, around a mouthful of spaghetti. He gives another jerk, like someone has kicked him, and glares. "I swear to Noblar, do that again."

Gabe comes over and takes Bennie's plate. "Come along. We have things to do that aren't here. You can eat there." He turns and starts to leave, Bennie's dinner in one hand.

Bennie lets out a growl-like noise, turns to Wil and glares, then hops out of the seat and follows Gabe. As they near the hatch leading to engineering, Wil can hear him complain, "You said I couldn't eat in engineering anymore."

"I will make an exception, this one time," the tall droid says, looking back at Wil and Cynthia, now alone in the lounge.

"I think he thinks you and he are competing for my affections," Cynthia says in a low voice, smiling behind her drink.

Wil feels his face warm up. "Oh, uh. Hmm. Are we?" His face feels so hot he's sure it must be red as a beetroot.

"You're kind of horrible at this," Cynthia laughs, scooting closer to him on the bench.

"So yeah, you never answered my question?" he protests weakly.

"About how I ended up working for Xarrix? It's not that interesting a story really. I was working for Lorath as her second in an extortion racket in one of the larger night markets on Fury, when Xarrix took notice and absorbed her operations. Rather than get herself killed, she became his second, and I stayed on as hers."

Wil jumps slightly, feeling a hand on his thigh. "Oh... uh," he says, a few octaves higher than normal. "When I met you were her secretary."

"A convenient cover. I sat out there, in case any nosy official or anyone else popped their head in. We didn't get many visitors, and those we did we were usually expecting, like you." She smiles broadly, her very sharp-looking incisors gleaming. "Though I'll admit, we weren't expecting the Peacekeepers to be following you."

He affects a stricken look. "Hey, they weren't following me, they raided you lot separately." The pressure on this leg moves up slightly.

"Uh, huh," she says, smiling slyly.

MOVIE NIGHT

"The *Huflo* is docking now," reports Zephyr, looking up from her screen to the image on the main display. On it, several of the small salvage vessels have latched themselves on to one of the larger derelicts. The larger *Plo* is also sliding into position alongside the derelict, guided by the smaller tugs.

"I guess now we wait," Wil says, spinning in his chair. "How's the B team doing?"

"According to scans, about the same, their salvagers have just docked. "

"PASS ME MORE OF THAT, WHAT DID YOU CALL IT? POPCORN?" Cynthia says, reaching across Wil, who's next to her on the sofa in the lounge. Maxim is on her other side, with Zephyr next to him. Gabe, now that his frame shares proportions similar to his crew mates, is in the large chair next to the sofa. He takes the popcorn from Bennie, who has taken to sitting on the arm of the chair when Gabe joins them, and with a series of clicks and slight whirs extends his arm several feet, over to Cynthia, who is staring wide-eyed.

"I didn't know he could do that," she says in awe.

Wil shakes his head smiling. "Neither did we. Gabe is full of surprises lately." He presses a button on his wristcomm, and the movie pauses. "Where'd you pick that up?"

Gabe retracts his arm, which makes soft clicking sounds as it settles back into place. He lifts his hand to inspect it, rotating it one hundred and eighty degrees. "As I mentioned on Fury, I have been experimenting with this new body. The design I based myself on seems to be tremendously adaptable." Shrugging, he adds, "There is, however, no instruction manual."

Cynthia leers at the engineering bot. "Exactly how adaptable are we talking here?" She raises her eyebrows, her feline ears twitching.

"Down, girl," Wil says, resting a hand on her knee. From the other side of Maxim, there's a low rumble. Wil presses the control on his wristcomm, and the movie resumes.

Bennie leans forward. "So this is called what again?"

Without taking his eyes off the screen, Wil answers, "*Ghostbusters.*"

Zephyr reaches over and takes the popcorn from Cynthia. "I like that the main characters are all women." Cynthia nods, which only irritates Zephyr.

Wil nods. "There's an older version, it's just as great. We can watch it next movie night and you guys can compare. I like this one a lot, but both are pretty awesome."

"What is the role the blonde male serves?" Cynthia asks. "I mean, he is quite attractive for a human, but he seems mentally deficient."

"He's the secretary, or I guess, he's supposed to be. I think they intentionally made him dumb as a brick as a bit of social commentary," Wil explains.

"I see," Cynthia replies, thinking. She turns to Wil. "I prefer brown hair." Her grin highlights her sharp incisors.

Maxim coughs once, then gestures to the screen. "Those

weapons look quite powerful." On screen, one of the characters is destroying an alleyway with her out-of-control weapon. "This is, what did you call it? Slapstick?"

Wil clears his throat, reaching for his drink. "Uh, oh, yeah. More or less. Physical comedy like this was pretty popular when this movie came out. I was pretty young, but the main characters were in several movies with similar antics. Oh, there's a funny dance sequence in this too."

"I do not understand why in the middle of battle, anyone would choose to… dance," Gabe remarks.

Bennie shakes his head. "This is a comedy. Sort of like *Quiznar and the Wonkins*, but you know, with humans."

"I see," Gabe says. His face, now more emotive than before, says otherwise.

"And *Ghosts*," Bennie offers.

"I was an engineering bot on a Peacekeeper command carrier. I did not watch entertainment vids."

"Didn't the engineers have a break room?" Zephyr asks.

Gabe nods. "Droids were not allowed in the break room."

Everyone finds something else to look at.

On the screen two of the characters are now dressed all in black, doing an interpretive dance. Gabe stands. "I will be in engineering."

ALWAYS WITH THE SECRETS

"First derelict looks like it's on the move," Zephyr reports. On the screen, the derelict the *Huflo* had been docked with is lurching slightly and moving off toward a section of space near the *Berserker*. Jurrella wants each ship to take up a position around her flagship once it is online. The newly reactivated vessel is moving like its pilot is drunk.

From her now-usual spot at one of the aft stations of the bridge, Cynthia's wristcomm beeps. She looks down. "Go ahead Lorath," she says. There is a pause. "One second." She stands, looks at Wil, then Zephyr, then leaves the bridge.

As the hatch closes, Wil looks over at Bennie, who has already turned in his seat, waiting for Wil to look at him. He nods. Bennie grins and turns back to his console. Wil taps a few controls on his chair, and one of the smaller displays on his console comes to life— a wireframe of the ship appears, with a blinking yellow dot moving down the long corridor that connects the forward section of the ship to the larger main body. They watch as the dot moved all the way to Cynthia's quarters.

"Why that sexy flobin," Bennie mumbles.

Everyone turns to Bennie. Wil says, "I'm sorry, what now?"

Bennie looks up. "She has a scrambler, a good one, in her quarters." He looks at the ceiling, mimicking Wil's habit. "Gabe, can you help me with this?"

"What do you need?" the ceiling asks.

"There's a scrambler in use in Cynthia's quarters—"

From the overhead speakers, "Of course, one moment."

Bennie turns his attention back to his console, mumbling a little here and there, then Gabe is back on the speakers. "Did that help?"

Bennie smiles. "It did, yeah. Well, at least a little." He presses a button.

The speakers come to life, "—let them find out—" something, something, some garbled back and forth, "—biotech warfare division will pay handsomely—" This is followed by a burst of static. Wil looks over at Bennie, who is frantically working at his console. "—Do what you have to do—" a little more static, "Xarrix doesn't care," then Cynthia's voice, "I can take care of it."

Zephyr is staring at Bennie. "That's it? Seriously what do we even keep you around for?"

"Harsh," Maxim says, under his breath.

"Grolack off!" Bennie shouts. "If I'd known she had a scrambler, I could have planned for it. Wil, you didn't see anything like that last night? Or the night before?"

"Come again?" Zephyr says, turning slowly to face Wil. The look on her face a cross between betrayal and disgust, but mostly disgust.

Wil can feel the heat rising from his neck to his cheeks. "Uh, no, didn't see anything… but also don't know what a scrambler looks like, so you know, there's that." He turns to fully face Bennie. "And you know, fuck you dude! Not cool!" Maxim is trying and failing to stifle his laughter. Zephyr is staring at Wil, her mouth hanging open. Wil spins his chair back to face Zephyr and Maxim. "Okay, moving on." He looks at Maxim deadpan. Maxim is still trying really hard to not fall over laughing, but the ex-Peacekeeper just rests one hand on his console, shaking his head a few times, then looks at Wil and gives him what Wil knows is the Palorian equivalent of a thumbs-up. "Moving on, what was all that? Biotech division? Whose? Do whatever it takes? Does she have weapons on board?"

"I searched her and her belongings when she came aboard," Maxim offers, then grins at Wil. "I suppose I could have let you search her, you know, more thoroughly." He chuckles.

Wil flips him off. "Did anyone search her when she came from the *Berserker* last time?"

Zephyr looks at Maxim, who is now dead serious. Both shake their heads. Wil looks at Bennie, who stares back at him, face completely blank. "That's a no, then."

"I hate that flobin," Zephyr mumbles. She looks at Wil. "We can talk about your life choices later."

Wil grimaces, then looks at the ceiling. "Gabe?"

"Yes, Captain."

"Scan—"

"What's going on? Is something wrong?" Cynthia says, as she walks on the bridge and hears Wil. In the confusion and embarrass-ment, he hadn't noticed her leave her quarters and begin walking back to the bridge—none of them had.

"—the outer hull, see if you can pick up the source of the weird lag I see on the starboard maneuvering thrusters."

A pause, then, "Of course, Captain."

"Is the ship okay?" the feline -featured maybe assassin asks, taking her seat.

Wil nods his head. "Oh, yeah. But since we're just sitting here, I figured I'd have him check out a weirdness I've been noticing. How's Lorath over on the SS Lilliput?"

The Tygran woman makes a face, then waves her hand. "She's fine, we had to discuss some business we left behind on Fury." She grins, showing her impressive incisors again. "Work never stops, you know."

"Don't I ever," Wil says, turning back to look down at his console.

CHAPTER XI

DISGRUNTLED EMPLOYEES

"The *Nuy'et'lu* is under attack!" Zephyr shouts over the overhead speakers. "Everyone to the bridge!"

Wil and Maxim drop their sandwiches and rush out of the lounge, followed by Cynthia, who's already reaching for her wrist-comm as she moves.

"Wait for me!" Bennie shouts, grabbing Maxim's sandwich off the table as he passes.

"What's going on, who's attacking? Which ship is the nut-loo?"

"*Nuy'et'lu*, and it's in the team B group of salvagers," Zephyr reports, vacating Wil's seat and moving to take her own.

Dropping down into his command station, Wil glances at his first officer. "Then what's the alert for? Follux Sul and his band of pirates can do what they're being paid to do."

"Apparently there are too many attackers," Maxim says, consulting his tactical station screens. He taps a control and the main display updates, changing to a tactical view with data, which Wil presumes has been provided by Sul's *Butcher*. On it, there are five red triangles, one green circle, the *Butcher*, and five yellow squares representing the salvager team. The yellow squares are moving away as fast as they can, in various random-seeming directions.

"Gabe, combat time!" Wil says to the ceiling, as he pushes the sub-light engine throttle control forward, forcing the *Ghost* to almost its full sub-light speed.

"Acknowledged, Captain."

From his station, Maxim reports, "Weapons hot."

Wil nods tersely. "Open a channel to the *Butcher*." He turns to Cynthia. "Let your boss and our salvagers know what's up, in case they don't already know." Cynthia nods and starts whispering into her wristcomm. "By the way, what's the *Berserker* doing?"

"The *Berserker* is turning toward the attack, but that thing is slow as grolack," Maxim reports.

A soft beep sounds, indicating that the *Butcher* has finally accepted the comms request. "Captain Noble-pants, I'm a little busy. What do you need?" Wil can hear Follux Sul's crew shouting to each other in the background. Something explodes somewhere on the small pirate's bridge.

"We're a few centocks out, keep 'em busy, and we'll pick a few off as we come in."

"I do not need your help, human—" static erupts on the channel, drowning out Sul for a moment, "—*Butcher* is more than capable of dealing with these grolacking flobins."

"Sure you can, Captain Lollypop Guild." Wil makes a slicing motion. A beep announces that Zephyr has closed the channel, and Wil turns to Maxim. "Max, what's your assessment?"

"Based on the telemetry data we're getting from the *Butcher*, all five vessels are mid-sized cutters. Individually, no match for either ship, especially his. But together, they pose a moderate threat, as the *Butcher* is finding out." The main display updates, showing a close-up view of the battle taking place ahead of them: on the screen the newer model Ankarran Raptor is venting something from one of its nacelles and its rear shields are down twenty percent. A medium-sized blaster turret deploys from between the sub-light engines, belching high energy plasma at one of the pursuing cutters.

"I want one of those," Wil says, watching the pursuing cutter fire a few more times before breaking off its pursuit, its own shields glowing from the intense fire they have absorbed.

"Looks like two of those cutters are sporting upgrades." Maxim gestures, indicating two of the five vessels that are more dangerous than the rest. "That one, and this one." The corresponding icons have changed to a darker red and become five-pointed stars instead of triangles.

"Guess we know who to target first. Send a tight-beam to the *Butcher*, let them know we're about to take out..." Wil thinks, then points, "that one."

"Done," Zephyr announces. "For all the good it will do."

The *Ghost* is burning hard, so Wil cuts her engines so that they're coasting, very fast, into the battle space. The larger and very much slower *Berserker* is still several minutes from even being close enough to lay down supporting fire and cover the *Ghost* and her newer-model cousin, the *Butcher*.

The moment the *Ghost* is in range, Maxim unleashes a volley of missiles from the launchers beneath the ship. Wil brings the *Ghost* in fast, only firing the retro thrusters as they swing through the mass of fighting vessels, sending three of the attackers scattering—including their target, one of the more upgraded cutters.

"Target has sustained damage," Maxim reports, over the sounds of the engine nacelle-mounted blaster cannons firing. "Another missile salvo should do it if they'll hold still." He turns slightly in his seat. "Also, Bennie, I know that's my sandwich, and when this is over if there isn't a newly made sandwich on my plate in the dining area, I will squeeze you until your head pops off." Bennie has a mouthful of the sandwich in his cheeks when he turns to Maxim, trying to reply around chews.

Wil grins, *Ah family*, as he brings the ship around in a tight arc that a pursuing cutter can't match. "I can take care of that."

Just as the *Ghost* is lining up to make another run on the upgraded cutter, it explodes.

"The hell?" Wil says, as on screen the *Butcher* blasts through the expanding debris cloud, flames from the destroyed cutter lingering on it, before vanishing in the vacuum. "That bastard!" Wil shouts, bringing the *Ghost* around, as several blaster bolts strike their shields from another of the attacking cutters.

"Starboard shields down five percent," Zephyr announces, gripping the side of her console as Wil brings the *Ghost* into a maneuver tight enough that the inertial dampers don't adequately compensate. The hull groans in protest, as does everyone on the bridge.

"Captain..." Gabe says over the speakers.

"She'll hold together," Wil says through gritted teeth, his vision graying slightly.

"It is not the ship I am worried about."

NEVER TRUST PIRATES

"Incoming, port side!" Zephyr shouts, as one of the attacking cutters emerges from around one of the dormant ships, its blasters raking the *Ghost's* shields.

Wil brings the ship hard to starboard, driving towards the attacking ship so Maxim can fire the forward blasters, before diving under the same derelict. On the main sensor display, the *Butcher* is giving chase to the ship they just exchanged fire with, destroying it.

"That son of a bitch keeps taking our kills. What the hell?" Wil checks the tactical display, seeing that there are only two of the attacking cutters left.

"It's not a contest," Cynthia says from behind Wil.

"Shows what you know," he growls, twisting the controls.

"The *Berserker* is on station! They're opening fire." Zephyr announces.

"About damn time," Bennie says, glancing over at Cynthia, who has been sitting at her station monitoring the battle.

She turns to him. "Don't look at me, little green, it's not like I'm in charge over there."

"You're not in charge anywhere," Zephyr says, not bothering to look over.

Wil growls again, bringing the *Ghost* around towards one of the last two attacking vessels. "That asshole isn't getting this one. Max," and Wil glances over briefly before turning his full attention to the other craft. The cutter has turned to put distance between itself and the *Berserker*. Its aft weapons are still blasting the *Ghost's* forward shields.

"Firing," Maxim reports, as two missiles streak up from the bottom of the main display, followed by several bright energy bolts from the nacelle and bridge-mounted blasters. The weapons fire converges, and the cutters shields flare, then fail, an explosion ripping apart the ship.

"Boom!" Wil shouts, thrusting one fist in the air.

An awkward minute passes before Maxim reports, "The last cutter looks like it's being brought aboard the *Berserker*."

"Incoming comms, the *Berserker*," Zephyr announces a moment later.

The main display changes, to show Xarrix. "The Duchess would like you aboard the *Berserker* for the interrogation."

"Interrogation?" Wil asks, looking back at Cynthia, who shrugs.

On the large screen Xarrix shrugs too. "She's paying us, we do what she wants. Be here in one-half tock."

DO UNTO OTHERS

"Well, this is kind of dark," Wil mutters, as he and Cynthia walk into the large lounge that had been the site of the massive feast and now looks like a medieval torture chamber. In the center of the room is a device that looks like something from ancient Europe back on Earth: there are straps, bars and chains all over it.

Cynthia moves to take a seat next to Lorath, who's on the far side of Follux Sul.

"What do you see?" Maxim asks, over the comm-link Wil has in his ear. After the last visit, the crew had agreed they wanted to have at least ears in the room when Wil was aboard the *Berserker*. The link is paired to his wristcomm, just like the old Bluetooth headset he used to have on Earth.

"Some kind of weird looking do-dad in the middle of the room. Jurrella's throne is where it was last time, but now there're like… bleachers, or something set, up." Wil walks over to Xarrix, who motions for him to sit down. On Xarrix's other side is Follux Sul, who makes what Wil assumes is a rude gesture on his world. He leans over to speak to Xarrix. "What the hell is this?"

The reptilian crime lord shrugs. "Apparently our client—"

"Your client." Wil corrects.

"—my client, has a bit of a theatrical streak."

Wil decides to change the subject. "So what're these derelicts exactly? They seem to take a bit of work to get up and running."

A shrug from Xarrix. "They're an old design. Once the salvagers get the hang of it, things should speed up. Why? Do you have better places to be?"

"Other than away from you and this," Wil gestures to the room around them, "freak show, no, not really."

From the opposite entrance that Wil and everyone else had come through, Jurrella and two guards stride in, followed by what looks like two droids and two Quillant.

"What the hell?" Wil whispers.

"What is it?" Zephyr asks.

From behind Zephyr, Wil can hear Bennie. "We should have added a camera."

"To what? his forehead?" Wil can hear Maxim retort.

Wil coughs to get his crew's attention. "Must be the crew of the cutter—two Quillant and two droids. One looks like a light-duty engineering bot, and one is a model I've never seen: four eyes, two arms, two legs, kinda big head, flat, matte black, eyes are huge."

"An intelligence and command droid," Gabe offers. "They're typically assigned to front-line Peacekeeper platoons as liaisons to division commanders. They are tremendously loyal and incredibly intelligent. I wonder how this one was enticed to join a pirate organization?"

The smaller engineering droid is being led by two additional guards toward the device in the center of the room. The droid's design is similar to Gabe's original body, but shorter and lacking the extra set of smaller utility arms.

Jurrella takes her seat, and gestures to the droid being attached to the device. "These vermin are the crew of the vessel we captured." The crowd, most of whom must be her crew and the same various hangers-on that Wil saw before, all cheer.

"I have a bad feeling about this," Wil mumbles. Xarrix turns his head slightly, looking at Wil askance.

Jurrella leans forward on her throne. "Did Bunto hire any more ships? Where are they? Where is Bunto?"

"Mr. Bunto hired five vessels, with crews," one of the Quillant offers from beside the device the droid, clearly terrified, is hooked up to.

The warlord duchess nods to one guard, who grabs the Quillant and drags him forward. "How—many—ships did he hire?"

"I—I told you!" the terrified alien screams, the catfish-like whiskers around its mouth twitching.

Jurrella presses a control on her throne, and one section of the device begins to move—it pulls the engineering droid's arms right out of their sockets, spraying purple fluid everywhere, sparks flying from the damaged sockets. The Quillant falls to his knees, making a high-pitched keening sound.

"Jesus!" Wil exclaims, jumping to his feet.

A reptilian hand grabs his. "Sit. Down." Wil does.

"This is barbaric!" he hisses at Xarrix. The Trenbal crime boss nods once, not taking his eyes off the spectacle.

One of Jurrella's guards walks up to the sobbing Quillant, pressing a pulse pistol to its temple. The whiskers twitch as it cries out.

Jurrella looks around the room. "Bunto hired this drennog to take what is mine!" The crowd in the room roars its anger. She nods, and the guard fires one shot.

As the guards remove the body, the matte-black intel droid speaks up. "He was telling you the truth. Mr. Bunto contracted five cutters and crews from my owner. I was assigned to liaise with Mr. Bunto and ensure my owner's property was returned in as good of shape as possible." The droid looks around the throne room. "It would appear that I have failed. Mr. Bunto was on the *Spurlok,* which was destroyed.

After removing the engineering bot from the device, the guards grab the intel bot and drag it to the middle of the room. The engineering bot seems to be functional, barely. Its optic sensors are still glowing, but it is otherwise not moving or doing much of anything, as far as Wil can tell.

"Xarrix, this is bullshit," Wil says, leaning over to the Trenbal.

"What's going on? We heard screaming," Zephyr says over the comms.

Wil looks back toward the center of the room ,where the engineering droid is strung up in the torture device. "Not now." He glances over to Follux Sul, who turns and smiles at him, a jewel-encrusted smile.

Jurrella gets up from her throne and strides down to the center of the room. She raises her arms, and spins to take in the audience. "This robot would take from us what is ours! Bunto, who started this journey with us, would take from us that which is ours! That which we've worked so hard, and so long for!" The crowd erupts into cheers and shouts.

"What is she talking about?" Wil asks Xarrix.

EVERYTHING IS NOT OKAY

As Jurrella works the room into a frenzy, Xarrix begins to explain. "I take it you know little about the Werdlow system." Before Wil can answer, he continues, "When the Peacekeepers gave up trying to pacify this system, they not only left but took their toys with them. The residents of the planet found themselves suddenly on their own—deservedly, some would argue. They had to learn to farm and trade with the few traders who'd visit the planet."

"He's right," Zephyr whispers in Wil's ear.

"Jurrella's family united most of the colonies on the planet," Xarrix continues, "by force when necessary, but usually it wasn't. Her father and grandfather were charismatic leaders." He gestures toward the Duchess, still working the crowd, while the trussed-up intel bot watches. The remaining Quillant is standing silently between two guards, its eyes unfocused.

Follux Sul turns and hisses, "Would you two gossips like to take your chat outside? The show is getting good!"

Wil flips him off, just as Jurrella stops before the intel bot. "You worked for the enemies of Werdlow! You took part in an attack that could have cost our world its freedom and prosperity!"

"I repeat, I am only—"

Jurrella motions to one of her guards, who activates the device which immediately separates the droid's limbs from its body. It emits a low warbling kind of sound.

"What was that?" Bennie asks over the comms.

"She just ripped the droid's arms and legs off," Wil says under his breath, so as not to alert anyone to his comms device.

"She is torturing her," Gabe says matter-of-factly.

"Her?" Wil whispers in unison with Zephyr.

"The intonation of her voice suggests she has affected a female persona. She answered the Duchess' question honestly," Gabe informs them.

As the body of the droid slumps to the ground, held up by a few stray wires coming from its now separated limbs, the crowd once again erupts in cheers. The droid's optical sensors flutter before going dark.

Xarrix leans over. "Her father purchased this ship with the entire savings of the colony. They used it to run freight at first, then to pirate when it was safe to do so. Every credit they stole and earned went to the colony, and they sold every unit of production and refined goods the colony could produce to fill the coffers. Jurrella learned of the derelict fleet from her cousin, Bunto. Apparently, Bunto wanted to sell the ships."

"And she wanted to build both a maritime and military fleet, with your help," Wil finishes.

"What's happening?" Bennie pushes.

The remaining Quillant crew member is standing before the remains of the intel bot. "Was Bunto operating alone?" Jurrella asks. "He and his thieving mate Wi'Qu left together."

"I never met any Wi'Qu," the captive replies, trembling. It is wringing its hands worriedly.

"You lie!" the Duchess shouts, encouraging the crowd to scream at the captive, who shrinks back against the verbal onslaught. Without a word, one of her guards walks up and shoots the Quillant in the back of the head.

"God!" Wil says. Then, to head off his team's questions, he whispers, "She just executed the other Quillant."

Jurrella turns to the crowd, then points to the last survivor of the failed attack, the arm-less engineering bot. "This one will fight! Tonight!"

"Fight?" Maxim asks.

"Fight?" Wil asks Xarrix.

"A popular pastime on Werdlow Three is droid fights," the crime boss replies offhandedly.

"That's not okay," Wil grinds out. "It doesn't even have arms."

"Yes, that will be a handicap for sure. You're welcome to stand up and tell her that. I trust your crew is prepared to carry on the assignment without you? Though, given what we've just seen, she may just torture and kill them all, except your droid. She'll make him fight, he's too unique to just destroy outright." Xarrix pauses to think. "She might sell him though, he really is unique."

Wil growls and gets up. "This is grolacked!" He makes his way toward the exit, while Jurrella watches.

CHAPTER XII

THINGS WE DON'T THINK ABOUT

"Gabe is pouting," Maxim says, as Wil closes the airlock door behind him, having thankfully left the *Berserker* behind.

"Can't say I blame him. This mission just took a kind of dark turn." Wil slips the earpiece back into a pocket on his jumpsuit. "Let's put some distance between us and this nightmare. We can take our salvagers out to the far end of the flotilla."

Maxim nods. "I'll get us going, you go check on Gabe." He can see Wil take a big breath and exhale, then nod.

"CAN I COME IN?" WIL ASKS, AS THE DOOR TO ENGINEERING SLIDES open.

"Of course, Captain. It is your ship." The engineering bot's voice comes from somewhere behind the main engine.

"How are you doing, big guy? That must have been rough to hear, you know, back aboard the *Berserker*." Wil takes a few tentative steps into the engineering space, letting the hatch close behind him.

"To be honest, Captain, it was nothing I have not encountered before. Except for a few minor, outlying colonies, droids do not have civil rights. We are routinely tortured for sport and treated as property to be abused as desired, and discarded when too damaged for any use."

As Wil comes around the reactor, he sees a space he doesn't recall ever seeing before. It is a small maintenance workstation that's been reconfigured into what he can only call a bedroom—though sans bed. Gabe is sitting on a bench against the far wall, the glow from the reactor illuminating his new, more expressive face.

Sitting down next to his robotic friend, Wil rests his hand on Gabe's shoulder. "I didn't know how bad it was." He shrugs. "I guess I never really paid any attention, I mean, before meeting you. Droids were always just in the background going about their business. I never considered—"

"You would not be the only one. Few consider my kind anything but tools with minds." Gabe turns to look at Wil, his eyes clearly expressing sadness. *Damn, his new face really does convey his emotional state*, Wil thinks.

Wil pauses for a moment. "I guess it was easy for me to not see it. Lanksham didn't have any droids on the crew, and most of the places we went, droids were a luxury few could afford." He thinks a bit more. "I think my first real encounters with droids came after I was on my own." He shrugs. "By then I had other things on my mind."

Gabe says nothing, so Wil continues, "We'll fix this. We've got some clout with Harrith, maybe they can help put pressure on the GC. Start getting the conversation started. Hell, *we* have some clout with the GC too, though I haven no idea how to apply it."

"That is kind of you, Captain. I do not have much hope of anything like that succeeding. Droids have been a disposable workforce in the GC for over one hundred and fifty standard years. I do not see that changing anytime soon."

"That was before I got involved." Wil smiles and pats his friend's leg. "Also, at least using Earth as a model, change like this is slow—often way too slow." He smiles again. "What say we get this job done, get paid and never see Xarrix or the nut job Jurrella again, and set about fighting some civil rights fights?"

"I would like that." Gabe stands and follows Wil out of engineering.

As they cross through the lounge towards the hatch leading to the bridge, Wil asks, "Did the Peacekeepers mistreat you, or any of their droids for that matter?"

Gabe turns his head, looking down at Wil. "Sometimes, but not often. It was common to re-program the inhibitor key and force droids to fight each other for sport."

"Inhibitor key?"

"The inhibitor key is a device inside each droid. It is essentially the ownership key. Once keyed with specific command codes and inserted into a droid, the droid cannot override anything contained on the key." Tapping on his chest, Gabe adds, "Droids are also unable to remove their or another droid's key."

"Do you have one?" Wil leans forward, eyeing Gabe's chest.

"I did. The ensign who smuggled me off the Command Carrier removed it, for some reason. I suspect it was part of his agreement with Xarrix. Had it been present when I powered on, I would have attempted to escape and return to the Peacekeepers by any means necessary." He smiles at Wil. "When I created this body, I did not include an inhibitor key port."

Wil nods, smiling back. "Smart."

Gabe nods. "Yes."

PILLOW TALK

"Are all humans like you?" Cynthia asks from beside him, this time in his quarters.

"What do you mean? Exceptional in bed?" Wil grins. "The answer is no." He thinks a bit, then adds, "But also, no in general. We come in lots of colors, sizes, and shapes. Different political leanings, religious leanings. Come to think of it, we're more unalike than anything. Sometimes for the worse."

She tuts. "I meant messy." She gestures to the rest of the room. "You're a grown man."

"Ouch!" He looks around. "But fair. I've slacked a little on the cleaning thing. I've been a bit pre-occupied."

She slaps a hand against his chest. "No excuse. You can't have people over and expect them to not be grossed out."

"You don't seem to mind—" Wil grunts, as a sharp furry elbow strikes his ribs. "Okay, no argument. I'll clean the place up."

"So, your world isn't united under one government?"

Wil laughs. "Oh god, no. I mean, we've made strides: the United Nations is the strongest it's ever been, but there are still plenty of non-aligned nations. Some out of disinterest, others because they have desires to overthrow the more powerful nations."

"If the GC ever approach your people, you know the planet has to be united under a single planetary government?" Cynthia says.

"Yeah, I think Earth is a long way from GC membership." He shrugs. "Who knows though, maybe finding life outside our system would be the kick in the pants humanity needs to get its act together." When his companion doesn't answer, Wil changes gears. "Does the treatment of droids bother you?"

"Wow, this took a turn." She turns and props herself up on an elbow. "Sort of. My planet, Tyr, has laws that give synthetic intelligence—droids—certain civil rights."

"I didn't know that. Gabe mentioned that certain worlds were like that, but not enough."

"He's not wrong. What you saw on the *Berserker* isn't that uncommon, especially on the more backwater worlds like Werdlow Three. The GC has done an outstanding job of keeping droids from getting even the smallest of rights. Companies like Farsight and other droid manufacturers certainly aren't helping either." Sighing, she looks Wil in the eyes. "Why?"

"I had an earpiece in last time I was aboard the *Berserker*. The crew heard almost everything."

"Gods you're dumb—"

"Hey—" Wil starts, but a fur-covered finger covers his lips.

"If Xarrix or Jurrella had caught on, it'd be you on that rack. Not to mention the trauma you likely caused your metal friend."

"We don't keep secrets from each other." Then he shakes his head. "Yeah, Gabe took it really hard, I'm not sure what to do about it." He falls back on the bed, looking up at the ceiling. *That intake looks like it needs cleaning too*, he observes. He coughs once. "So, yeah, I need to ask you something."

She looks down at him, one cat-like ear quirked. "You switch topics like a Drunlop changes phases."

Wil makes a face, processing what she just said, then shrugs. "What's the deal with these ships? What's Xarrix up to? What are bio-weapons doing here and where are they?"

Now both ears are laying flat against her head. "What do you mean?"

"I—we, heard you talking to Lorath the other day."

"How? You hacked my quarters? Installed Surveillance?" She's out of bed now, grabbing clothes from the floor.

Wil sits up. "Can you blame us?" He spreads his hands. "Looks like it was warranted, after all. So what's up? There's more to this than salvaging some derelict ships."

As she opens the hatch to leave his quarters, she flips him off.

The hatch closes.

"That went well," Wil mumbles, looking for his pants.

"WHAT DO YOU MAKE OF ALL THIS?" MAXIM AND ZEPHYR ARE IN bed, both looking up at the ceiling. Maxim turns to look at his companion.

"Which *all of this* do you mean?" Her smile doesn't reach her eyes.

The big Palorian looks over at the love of his life. "Working for Xarrix, Gabe's reaction to what Wil saw aboard the *Berserker*..." He pauses. "... his relationship with Cynthia."

"Oh, *all* all of this." She hikes herself up on both elbows. "I don't really have a strong opinion on working for Xarrix. We take some jobs that are horrible and some that aren't. This is the former." She reaches for a glass of water next to her pulse pistol on the bedside table. After a sip, he continues, "The droid thing was bound to come up. Remember our discussion on Brai?"

"I do. Did I tell you I spoke with Gabe after leaving Brai?"

"You didn't." She gets up to walk to the bathroom and refill her glass. over the running water she asks, "How'd that go?"

"He gives me a run for my money in the stoic department, that's for sure. But since his... transformation... and his time aboard the *Siege Perilous*, he's been less droid-like. He said it was because he was able to strip away a lot of the programming Farsight forces on droids to keep them docile and subservient." Maxim lifts the covers so she can get back in bed. "I never really thought about that, that Farsight or the GC would put a code in place, to enforce their will on droids." He shrugs. "But I guess that makes sense."

When Zephyr doesn't say anything, he continues, "I know you don't like her, but is it really any of our business who Wil invites into his bed?" At her look of disgust he continues, "Besides, poor guy's been damn-near celibate for as long as we've known him. I'm surprised he hasn't gone insane."

Zephyr shakes her head. "Men."

ALWAYS SOMETHING

"Salvage Team A is docked," Zephyr announces, as the small fleet of freighters and salvagers latch on to the large derelict directly ahead. It is the twelfth derelict they've salvaged since starting the operation.

A cough from behind Wil causes everyone to turn. Cynthia is standing just inside the hatch. She looks down at her feet, then mumbles something.

"I'm sorry?" Wil says.

"She said, they're alive," Bennie offers.

Wil turns to him, the question clear on his face. The Brailack shrugs. "Just because humans have underdeveloped senses."

"You don't even have ears," Wil mutters, then turns back to Cynthia. "What're alive?"

"The ships," the Tygran woman answers.

"Not all of us advertise our sensory organs like humans do," Bennie quips.

"Oh dren," Maxim says. "We've been down this road before, recently."

Cynthia shakes her head. "Not like that dreadnaught thing. Like us."

"Come again?" Wil says.

"Is there a difference?" Zephyr asks.

Cynthia walks over and takes a seat at the station she's been occupying since the mission started. "They're biomechanical. Some type of giant creatures—living starships. We call them Behemoths, because of their size. They're in some type of hibernation state. The teams are going aboard and lobotomizing them, then taking manual control. That's why it's taken so long: the salvagers have had to map out the neural pathways as they cut them open."

"That's grotesque," Zephyr says, in a low voice.

"Truly," Wil agrees. "What the hell, Cynthia?"

She shrugs. "What you said last night got me thinking." She looks Wil in the eye. "I'm not okay with what they're doing. I wasn't before, but I've learned to not look too hard at what Xarrix gets into. I've been in this line of work so long I've gotten good at mentally separating myself from it." She smiles shyly. "I guess you're rubbing off on me."

"He does that," Maxim says. "A shower will help."

"Man, it's always something," Wil grouses. "Can't we have a few months of just boring ass work that pays well?"

"Emphasis on boring." Bennie says. "So, now what?"

Maxim looks from Wil to Cynthia, then at Bennie. "You have to ask? We stop this. The way we stop everything." He's grinning.

"By... blowing things up?" Wil asks. "I mean, we do blow things up a lot."

Maxim is nodding. "exactly."

Cynthia sighs. "I've been down this road before."

Wil laughs. "To be clear, I didn't cause your building to explode."

"Uh, huh."

"It was Lorath," Wil protests.

Zephyr clears her throat. "So, what do we do?"

"Let's go pay our boss and his boss a visit," Wil says, smiling.

"Docking clamps locked. Good seal on the airlock," Bennie reports from the bridge.

Wil looks at the group assembled in the armory; Zephyr, Maxim, and Cynthia. "Let's do this," he says.

Zephyr looks at Cynthia. "Don't shed in that armor—it's mine."

Cynthia makes a purring noise. "Explains why it's so big." Before Zephyr can react, the Tygran turns and heads towards the airlock.

Max and Wil exchange a look and follow after her.

Sitting on the bridge of the *Butcher*, Lorath's wristcomm vibrates a pattern she knows well. "Excuse me, Captain Sul." Without waiting for the diminutive pirate to answer, she gets up and leaves the bridge, thankful to be away from the pervasive smell of Follux Sul's first officer.

Entering her quarters, she lifts her arm, activating the comm link. "They know," Xarrix says from the small screen on her forearm. Sitting down at the desk set into the bulkhead, she swipes on the screen, and Xarrix's image moves to the larger display on the desktop unit.

"It was bound to happen, I suppose. Wil isn't nearly as dumb as he looks." The scaled second-in-command looks at her boss. "I wonder how, though?"

"Cynthia."

"Excuse me?" She leans toward the screen.

"Wil. That damned human corrupted her." Xarrix leans back. "She was such a valuable asset."

"How?"

"Slept with her." His face shows just how disgusting the idea is to him.

"Dammit. I invested a lot in her training. That idiot owes us."

Xarrix smiles. "As it happens, we'll get to exact a price for the loss of our associate, sooner rather than later. They're planning to storm the *Berserker*."

"Bold. Surely Wil knows how many armed guards and mercenaries are on board?"

"He does, or at least he should, having been aboard, but..." Xarrix makes an expansive gesture. "...humans."

"I hope they don't leave their home system anytime soon. Gods help us all."

"Indeed. At any rate, it's time to contain our band of misfits, it seems."

"Understood." Lorath reaches over to the terminal and brings up a menu. On it is the *Ghost* and the *Butcher*. She selects the former, and activates a command. "I'll assemble a crew."

CHAPTER XIII

BREAKING AND ENTERING

As they exit the armory, the lights in the small corridor between it and the airlock dim, then go out. "Uh." Wil looks at the ceiling. "Hey Gabe, did you power down the reactor?"

Maxim and Zephyr both look at Wil, as the red automatic emergency lighting activates.

"I did not, someone has infiltrated our systems. They are all shutting down."

Without a word, Zephyr is moving. She has her hands around Cynthia's throat before anyone, including Cynthia, can react. She moves to head butt the Tygran woman, only to slam her faceplate against Cynthia's own faceplate.

From the Ceiling, Bennie announces. "Everything is shutting down! I'm trying to counter, but... I don't know where it's coming from!"

Cynthia breaks Zephyr's hold and jumps against the wall to get up and over the stunned ex-Peacekeeper. Using her tail as a counterbalance, Cynthia lands on the balls of her feet and swiftly launches into a spinning kick to Zephyr's midsection.

Zephyr's training takes over, and she grapples the leg as it connects with her side, causing her to exhale loudly. She lashes out with a savage jab right to her opponent's chest, followed by an equally brutal, full-powered kick to the same place the punch just landed. Cynthia's armored form flies backward and collides with Wil and Maxim.

Maxim immediately drops to one knee and pins the already wriggling woman to the ground.

"Whoa whoa whoa!" Wil says, arms outstretched to try to hold the charging Zephyr back. The small corridor that circles the bridge and armory and connects the port and starboard airlock has never felt so cramped.

Zephyr roars, "She's betrayed us. Stop thinking with your lopar!"

Wil takes a second to process what Zephyr's just said. "Wait, what, no!" He motions for Zephyr to stand down. "I mean, yeah she probably did betray—"

"I didn't—" Cynthia stops as Zephyr growls and takes a step forward. She reaches up to remove her armored helmet. "I swear it."

Wil shakes his head. "She's worth more alive than dead." He looks down at the feline featured woman at his feet. "Probably." When she looks up at him, he looks away.

Standing, adjusting the borrowed armor, Cynthia says again, "I didn't betray you." She holds a hand up as Zephyr once again growls and leans forward. "However, my orders were to subdue you if ordered. There's a canister of nitrozene tied to the main air exchanger."

Wil glances at the ceiling. "Gabe?"

"I am on my way," the droid replies from wherever he is in the ship.

Cynthia reaches into her jumpsuit leg pocket, slowly removing a small remote. She hands it to Wil. "Lorath or Xarrix must have done something to the ship. I was to use this, but I'm guessing Xarrix, or Lorath, realized I'd betrayed their confidence."

"When?" Maxim asks.

Wil shrugs. "Neither has been aboard during this mission and—son of a bitch." He turns to Bennie. "Scour the main computer. I'm guessing a subroutine that's never run, just executed."

Everyone watches Bennie for a minute or two. "Well?" Maxim asks.

"You're welcome to come over and do this your—wait." The small hacker pauses, presumably looking intently at his console. "Well, I'll be." Everyone turns and heads immediately for the bridge, Maxim resting one armored and powerful hand on Cynthia's shoulder.

The bridge hatch opens, and Gabe walks in holding a canister that looks to Wil a lot like a pony keg from the old liquor store in Denver he'd visit in college. "I have successfully disconnected the nitrozene." Setting the canister down next to the hatch, Gabe approaches Bennie. "Can I be of assistance?"

Wil glares at Bennie. "Jesus, dude. You're supposed to be our hacker! How did you miss that? It's had to have been part of the computer since before you came aboard with them." He hitches a thumb over his shoulder toward Maxim. "Xarrix hasn't had access to the *Ghost* since he helped me outfit it for my trip home."

"He's nothing if not patient," Cynthia offers. "He likely had his people install the subroutine and bury it then, waiting for just the right time."

"The data stick," Zephyr says, turning her ire back to Cynthia, still firmly in Maxim's grasp.

"Damn. You're right, there was probably code on that stick that activated the sleeper code Xarrix implanted. Then it was simple enough to send a signal." Wil looks around the room, before casting his gaze on Cynthia. "I thought we had something."

Before anyone can reply, there's a loud thunk against the hull, followed by another.

"I believe we are being boarded," Gabe offers.

Wil grabs his pistol from the holster on his thigh. "Good thing we're already dressed." He places his helmet back on his head and secures the seals. He points at Cynthia. "Wait here." Then he points at Bennie. "Keep an eye on her."

Bennie squeaks. "Me?"

WELL THAT WENT WELL

"This is embarrassing," Wil says, sitting on the narrow bench of the *Ghost's* brig.

"I didn't know we had a brig," Maxim offers. Zephyr, who's laying against him on the floor, chuckles mirthlessly.

"I mean, really embarrassing," Wil continues. "Sure we're not some type of crack commando squad," he looks over to Maxim and Zephyr, "well, not all of us. But still. It's like we were rank amateurs. Like we weren't even prepared."

Bennie, who's leaning against Cynthia in the opposite corner, offers, "If it helps, they clearly had that planned." He gestures beyond the cell where Gabe is standing in the corner, his eyes dark. "It takes more than a simple EMP to shut him down, especially that new body of his."

"Xarrix has clearly been monitoring us for some time," Zephyr says. "That pulse shut down our armor like nothing. Wil's armor isn't even Peacekeeper, and it didn't fare any better. That was far too specific to be anything but pre-planned."

Before anyone can look at her or say anything Cynthia offers, "I had nothing to do with it. The nitrozene was my play, nothing else."

"So, what now?" Maxim asks. "I assume you have some override or something? It's your ship after all."

Wil gestures around. "Notice the lights? Still on backup power." The lighting in the small room is the same faint red of the emergency lights.

The doors open and Lorath enters. She glances at Gabe's inert form in the corner, then continues toward the cell. "You need a larger brig," she says. Her smile has no friendliness to it.

"It'll be just right when it's you in here," Wil says, standing and walking over to the door. "What's going on? What're you and Xarrix up to?" He looks her in the eye. "What're you doing with these creatures? What're you going to do with my ship? My crew?"

She turns to Cynthia, ignoring Wil. "I'm disappointed in you. After all, we've been through. You choose—" she gestures to Wil, "That?"

Bennie chuckles as Wil starts to turn red. "Excuse me?"

Still looking directly at her former lieutenant, Lorath continues. "You've worked for me for cycles. You are—*were*, third in command of Xarrix's entire operation, you had more power than many government officials." Again she glances at Wil. "He can't be that good."

As Wil starts to smile, Cynthia answers, "He's not. But he is noble. It's been a long time since I've met someone like him. Like them." She gestures to everyone in the cell.

"How's that working out so far?" Lorath scoffs. With that, she turns and leaves the room.

"WE'RE ALMOST HALFWAY DONE. CAN YOU KEEP THINGS UNDER control over there?" Xarrix asks, from the main display on the *Ghost's* bridge.

"They're in the brig, the droid is offline. It shouldn't be a problem." Lorath is sitting in Wil's command chair, surrounded by four of Follux Sul's crew, on loan from the *Butcher*.

The Trenbal crime lord nods. "Very well, then. I'll keep an eye on Sul, you keep the *Ghost* in position, protecting salvage team A. Now that the salvagers are familiar with the neurology of the vessels, the acquisitions will go quicker."

"Xarrix. Did you know these vessels, these creatures, were, in fact, living things?"

"Does it matter?"

Lorath tuts. "You know better than that."

He smiles. "I do, but we've already had one of our best operatives go soft, I had to be sure that number hadn't grown to two."

"As if." She reaches over and closes the channel. Looking around at her loaner bridge crew she says, "Well, let's go protect those salvagers." She picks up the small blue figurine of Kel and turns it over in one hand, looking at it appraisingly. "Junk," she mumbles, sitting back down at the console.

One of her borrowed crew looks over from the sensor station. "Do we get to steal their stuff when we're done?"

"Of course. Everything on this ship will be fair game once we've disposed of its previous occupants." The scales along Lorath's neck shift color, as she imagines putting a pulse pistol to Wil's head.

BUSTIN' OUT

"Captain, please wake up. Captain..." There's a small zapping sound.

"Sweet boneless Christ!" Wil hisses, waking from his sleep and rubbing his butt cheek. "What's going on? Bennie was that you?"

The groggy Brailack opens one eye and sees Wil rubbing the wound. "What? Like did I bite your butt? No, no, I didn't bite your butt, krebnack." He rolls over.

"It was me." Two small yellow circles are staring at Wil and the crew from beyond the bars of their cell.

"Gabe?" Zephyr says, waking.

"Affirmative."

Maxim sits up. "I thought you were offline."

"While the energy pulse was certainly powerful, it was insufficient to incapacitate me."

"It's been a day..." Wil says, getting to his feet as the droid approaches the door to the cell.

"Despite this new body, I am still an engineer, not a warrior. I decided to wait and see what Lorath and her associates did before acting."

"You could have let us know," Wil insists.

The bot shrugs, then grabs the lock and crushes it in one hand.

"Okay, now what?" Cynthia asks.

"Well for one, we leave your ass here, and Gabe bends the door or something to keep you contained," Zephyr all but snarls.

Before Cynthia can reply Wil holds up both hands. "Ladies. I get it, you hate each other. It's time to either get over it or at least set it aside. Cynthia has proven she's with us on this. She's on our side, Zee."

Zephyr straightens, mulls what Wil said over, then extends her hand to the feline ex-criminal secretary. "Okay, he's right. Truce?"

Cynthia grasps Zephyr's forearm. "Truce." She looks around, "Now, let's go make Lorath regret locking us up." Her grin makes Wil shudder.

Wil looks up at Gabe. "You still connected to the ship's computer?"

A shake of the head. "Negative. They have disabled the wireless network."

"Smart," Bennie says. "Lorath doesn't need it, and she probably assumed that if we got free, we'd use it."

Cynthia looks down at Bennie. "Don't underestimate her. She survived a long time before joining Xarrix. That's not easy, and even less so for a woman. She's ruthless."

Wil shudders, remembering his first meeting with Lorath, shortly after the crew stole the crate with Gabe in it for Xarrix. He'd sent his new team off on shopping errands, while he delivered the news that he would not, in fact, be providing the droid to Xarrix, or his proxy, Lorath. "Yeah, she is."

Zephyr eyes the hatch leading out of the brig. "Okay, so what's the plan?"

"I think I have an idea," Wil says, smiling.

Just then the *Ghost* lurches, then tilts wildly.

"THEY'RE A KILOMETER LONG, IT SHOULDN'T BE THAT HARD TO HIT them!" Lorath is shouting at the lanky Sylban occupying the weapons station.

Its wood-like limbs are moving over the controls. "This console is a mess!" it rattles in its rustling leaves-like voice. "Who configured it?"

"A Peacekeeper—hold on!" she shouts, banking the *Ghost* hard over to avoid an almost head-on collision with one of the smaller Behemoths. She glances at a Trenbal sitting at the sensor station— younger than Xarrix, a cousin if she recalls. "What's happening? Can you reach the salvage team?"

"I'm working on it!" the rattled reptilian replies, then at the expression on Lorath's face, adds, "Ma'am." A moment later, he says, "I have Captain Gub of the *Huflo*."

The overhead speaker beeps. "We're evacuating this one! There seems to be some type of defense mechanism—Aghh! Watch out Nolpe! Dammit!"

"What's going on over there, Captain!" Lorath shouts, watching the screen as the Behemoth that's been attacking them veers off and collides with another. "Captain Gub?"

The comms link is silent. Just as she turns to ask if they're still connected, it bursts into life again. "We're aboard the *Huflo*. You have to destroy this thing!" On the screen, the *Huflo* and two other salvage vessels detach from the wild Behemoth and jet away on different flight paths, engines flaring brightly at maximum thrust. One vessel isn't fast enough, shattering like glass against the thick space-being's hide.

"Target that thing!" Lorath orders the Sylban weapons officer. "Fire everything we have!" A moment later she can see several missiles appear at the bottom of the screen, arcing towards the Behemoth that is now turning back on to an intercept course with them. The first missiles impact against the armor-like outer skin, showing little sign of serious damage. Then the third missile strikes and in a blinding flash breaks the rogue living starship in half. "What the grolack was that?" she asks, turning to the Sylban.

"They have XPX-1900s," the wood-like alien says, possibly grinning—Lorath finds it hard to tell. "Well, they did."

Pressing a button, she says, "Captain Gub, the rogue vessel is destroyed. What happened?"

"Good to hear, thank you! One of my assistants cut the wrong fiber. Whatever it was, it almost immediately caused the creature to reactivate. We tried severing the connections like normal, but it activated internal defenses. Small creatures came out of nowhere—violent little yellow things, with blasters and other weapons attached to them, hundreds at once."

"Good to know, I'll make sure to pass your experience along to the other teams. Make sure your people are careful, Jurrella won't like that we've had to destroy one of her prizes." She's about to cut the connection, then adds, "Oh, and document which fiber your assistant cut so we can share that with the rest of the salvagers."

CHAPTER XIV

OPERATION: TAKE BACK THE SHIP. PHASE 1

Bennie is shaking his head. "That's your plan?"

"Yeah, what's wrong with it?" Wil asks, opening the hatch leading out of the brig a crack to peek down the corridor. The brig is just off the crew lounge, down a short hallway, and opposite the passage to the crews' quarters.

"Well for one, shoving me in the main ventilation duct is what's wrong with it." The scowl on the Brailack's face is almost comical to Wil. "What exactly, again, am I supposed to do?"

Maxim looks over from the opposite side of the door to Wil. "Make your way to the bridge, and be ready."

"Ready for what?"

Gabe grabs Bennie by his jumpsuit and lifts him as Maxim answers, "Anything." He motions Gabe through the hatch, closing it behind the bot and its captive Brailack.

Wil looks at Zephyr and Cynthia. "You two think you can keep from killing each other long enough to kill bad guys?" Zephyr rolls her eyes and pushes past Wil, followed by Cynthia. He looks at Maxim. "Ready?" The big Palorian cracks his knuckles. "Hopefully whatever they were doing earlier, they don't repeat."

"I don't like this," Bennie says, as Gabe removes the bolts holding the grate in place. The primary air handling system is served by a large conduit that runs the length of the *Ghost* and has branches to serve the various sections of the ship. It's the same system that Gabe recently uninstalled the nitrozene canister from.

Gabe looks down at his friend. "I believe the time for objections has passed."

Bennie raises a green eyebrow, or where eyebrows would be if he had them. "I objected then too."

Gabe shrugs, and reaches down for his friend. "Up you go."

As Gabe re-secures the bolts, he hears Bennie start working his way through the duct. "Try to be as quiet as possible."

"I hate you guys," comes the hissed reply.

"These smell." Cynthia's feline nose is twitching as she inspects one of the emergency spacesuits in the small room.

"Blame your boyfriend. I've been trying to get him to replace or at least clean them since I first found them," Zephyr replies, holding her own suit at arm's length as she undoes the zipper on the front. "Hopefully we won't be in them very long. You said the Behemoths have an atmosphere?"

Cynthia nods once. "That's what Lorath said, yes. Apparently part of their biological process, even in hibernation, is to produce oxygen."

Zephyr sits to don her boots. "They're all just dormant? How do they not wake up when the salvagers board?"

Cynthia shrugs. "We don't feel the germs that crawl around in and on us. From what I picked up from Lorath and Xarrix, these things have been drifting here for hundreds of cycles, in some sort of standby mode. Someone must have left them here and never come back." She gestures around the room. "This part of space is pretty desolate. Werdlow Three has only been colonized for five hundred cycles, after all."

"So on top of whatever ghoulish things are being done to these creatures, we're also stealing them," Zephyr says. Standing, she sighs. "Come on, let's do this." She reaches up and pulls a lever, causing a circular hatch in the ceiling to open. A similar hatch is visible a meter above it, then only space beyond.

"Handy little place, this," Cynthia says, looking around the room they're in.

Zephyr smiles, remembering when she and Maxim first met Wil, dropping down into the *Ghost* from the Partherian warship they were being held prisoner on. "It has its uses." She presses a button and the hatch leading into the room closes. "Helmets." She says, clicking her helmet in place on the neck on her suit. She presses another button, and the entire room decompresses, the oxygen being sucked out. She grabs two small thruster packs, handing one to Cynthia. "These should get us over there. After that, we'll have to figure something out."

Nodding, Cynthia takes the pack and puts it on.

One last button and the outer circular hatch opens. "Here we go," Zephyr says.

AFTER HELPING BENNIE GET INTO THE CENTRAL ATMOSPHERIC system, Gabe heads for engineering. His new sensor suite, courtesy of the mega-warship *Siege Perilous*, provides a warning when he needs to duck out of the way. Luckily it appears that Lorath has only a small crew with her.

Approaching the door, his sensors register three life forms inside the engineering compartment. Reaching for the button to open the hatch, his eyes shift from their usual yellow glow to a more menacing red.

"There," Cynthia says, as they approach the Behemoth. She's pointing at one of the salvager ships. "They leave the ships empty, it takes all of them to finish the task." She looks around. "What's all this debris?"

Zephyr adjusts her thrusters. "Not sure. It wasn't there earlier, must be what was causing the evasive maneuvers before."

"Looks like maybe one of the Behemoths," Cynthia offers. Zephyr nods. Several pieces of debris as big as the *Ghost* drift by.

"They don't take security very seriously, do they?" Zephyr asks, as the code-breaker software Bennie provided takes less than two seconds to open the outer airlock doors.

OPERATION: TAKE BACK THE
SHIP. PHASE 2

"R eady, pal?" Wil asks from outside the bridge.
Maxim nods. "Very."

Wil reaches down and presses a control. It beeps angrily and flashes red. "She's good." He reaches down and accesses a program on his wristcomm. "Bennie's better." He pulls a length of wire from the wristcomm, connecting it to the side of the access panel. Seconds later the wristcomm beeps, and the hatch control turns green. Putting the wire away, Wil presses the button, and the hatch opens.

Maxim rushes in first, followed by Wil.

THE HATCH TO ENGINEERING OPENS AND GABE STRIDES IN. THE moment he enters, he sees three Brailack in orange coveralls. "Hello."

Without a word and before he has a chance to act, all three rush the engineering bot, one leaping through the air and grappling Gabe's right arm. The other two tackle Gabe at the waist.

"Surely you do not think—" One of the waist-tacklers climbs up

Gabe's back and produces a plasma welder. Gabe reaches back for
the small attacker, but he dodges, and the one on his other arm
reaches around to grab onto his shoulder joint, producing a small
spanner.

"Oh, my..." Gabe says, mostly to himself, as his opponents don't
seem interested in dialogue. "I should have used my blasters."

"DO YOU KNOW WHERE WE'RE GOING?" ZEPHYR ASKS CYNTHIA, AS
they make their way through oddly organic corridors. They've only
encountered one scavenger so far, which they had to dispatch before
asking for directions. The corridors of the ship are more or less
uniform in their size, tall enough for an average-height being to
walk in and about two-and-a-half meters wide. Organic-looking
light fixtures are spaced about every meter.

"More or less. Lorath mentioned that their brains are forward
and near the center where the vessel is the widest. The corridors
should work their way there if it's that vital. Like a ship's bridge,
I think."

"She thinks..." Zephyr mumbles, just loud enough for her
partner to hear.

Cynthia stops and spins to face her. "Okay, look, what's your
problem? You have an interest in Wil? Hate Tygrans? What is it?"

"Wil? What? No, I'm with Maxim—wait, that's none of your
business. My problem," she begins ticking things off on her fingers,
"is that you're a criminal, an opportunist, a murderer, almost
certainly an assassin." Looking down at her hands, Zephyr realizes
she has one thumb left. "... and likely a backstabber."

Cynthia starts walking again. "First of all, you're no saint. You
think I don't know about the body count your little merry band
leaves behind?"

"Criminals, pirates, scumbags... mostly," Zephyr retorts.

"Secondly, you're a trained Peacekeeper intelligence operative. Your mate is a heavy weapons and tactics officer—"

"Ex-Peacekeepers."

Cynthia continues as if Zephyr hadn't interrupted: "...and small, green and annoying is a hacker with warrants throughout most of the GC. So yeah, I am an assassin, by training. Training that started when I was a kit, left on the street when Peacekeepers killed my mother. Training that replaced an orphanage and that replaced the likely end result of a penal colony, or work in a pleasure house. You're damn right I'm an assassin, or was." At the look Zephyr gives her, she adds, "I got out of that business as soon as I could, that's how I found myself in Lorath's employ. As for being a backstabber, I've been loyal to every employer I've ever had, until now." She looks at the Palorian woman, walking beside her. "What were your other super judgy points? I've forgotten."

Zephyr is silent for a few beats as they work their way through corridors, the signs of scavenger crews growing with each step. Trash is everywhere, and several sections of the passage are cut and pried open. Finally, Zephyr inhales. "I'm sorry."

"What's that? I didn't quite hear you?" Cynthia says, slowing as they approach a wide intersection.

"I judged you with incomplete information, which was more or less, *works for Xarrix*. That wasn't fair. Then you started to get close to Wil, and I was worried you'd hurt him when you betrayed him."

"Except I didn't betray him, or you, or hurt him."

"I know." Zephyr turns and puts a hand on the shoulder of her feline companion. "I'm sorry."

Cynthia nods. "Come on. I can hear the salvagers, we're close."

OPERATION: TAKE BACK THE SHIP. PHASE 3

"I hate them," Bennie mumbles to himself, as he inches his way through the primary ventilation shaft. "Treated like dren, made to crawl around in air ducts." He inches past something sticky and curses.

WIL AND MAXIM BURST THROUGH THE BRIDGE HATCH, CATCHING everyone inside by surprise. Lorath is the first to react, springing from the command chair toward the front of the bridge, far from the commotion. But as she does, her foot collides with the main controls, causing her leap to be less than graceful. The *Ghost* accelerates.

The Sylban at the weapons station lets out a rattling kind of scream, and the top of its head erupts in what looks to Wil like flowers.

The Trenbal occupying Zephyr's station turns to the intruders and leaps right at Wil, razor-sharp teeth bared. Before Wil can duck, a massive fist smashes into the side of the reptilian head, causing its owner to make a gurgling sound before collapsing to the deck, dead or unconscious.

The pair duck as blaster fire splashes over their heads, scorching several light fixtures and access panels. Wil grabs the blaster from the fallen Trenbal's holster and looks at Maxim. "You take tree guy." Maxim nods and crawls towards his station.

Wil stands and fires several shots, trying to not destroy the main display. "Give it up, Lorath!" He grabs the Kel figurine and hurls it at her.

She dodges the small blue projectile, swatting it away in mid-air. "Are you kidding? You'll be dead in a few centocks, then your big friend will join you. Then I'll track down his mate and that flobin Cynthia. I bet Xarrix lets me keep this ship as my personal transport." She stands and fires twice toward Wil, or at least where Wil had been.

Off to the side, Wil can see Maxim tackle the Sylban, which again lets out a strange rattling scream. This time, instead of its head blooming, large thorns emerge from its forearms. It swipes at the big ex-Peacekeeper, who dodges expertly, giving ground to the advancing alien.

Wil stands and fires just as Lorath is taking aim at Maxim. "Oh no you don't!"

She spins, returning her attention to Wil, and returns fire. "Once the four of you are dead, I'll sell that little green krebnack to someone who needs his services. There's always someone looking to influence an election or a stock market."

From above her head, comes a shout: "Like wurrin you will!" A grate drops from the ceiling, distracting Lorath enough that she doesn't see the small green blur shoot out of the duct. Bennie lands right on her face and starts raining blows with his small fists. "Sell me? Sell me? You sleazebag, lowlife—eep!" A scaled hand grabs his jumpsuit and hurls him across the bridge to collide with the central control console, his body smashing several controls. The *Ghost* tilts wildly.

Wil, already standing, fires once—hitting Lorath in the shoulder. "Don't make me—" he begins, but as she raises her weapon to fire, he shoots her in the chest. She is sent her flying against the main display screen, smearing blue blood against it. A smoking crater marks the dead center of her chest. Lorath looks up at Wil, then the life drains from her face and she collapses.

Wil hears a loud crack, like someone snapping a twig, and looks at Maxim just as he drops the Sylban to the deck. Cuts crisscross his arms and face, almost all of them bleeding. The big man shrugs. "Sorry, we didn't need prisoners, did we?"

Wil shrugs back. "Bodies are easier to get rid of." He looks over at Lorath's body. "This will really piss Xarrix off." He's smiling.

From the back of the bridge, a feeble voice asks, "Was that the signal?"

Wil laughs. "It sure was, pal." He walks over to his command chair and presses a button. "Gabe?" He looks down at the main controls and frowns.

Maxim leans down and helps Bennie up. "You were very fierce. Well done."

OVER THE SPEAKERS IN THE CEILING COMES WIL'S VOICE: "GABE?"

One of the Brailack engineers is laying in a heap near the reactor. The other two are still firmly attached to Gabe, who is spinning in circles as fast as he can while trying to grasp the fast-moving attackers. His left arm is shooting sparks out of the elbow joint while a section of his back plating is hanging loose.

"Go for its leg!" one of the attackers shouts.

As the Brailack clings to his back, dodging a swipe, it aims its plasma welder at his hip joint. Gabe lurches to one side, stopping his spinning just long enough to collide with one of the workbenches, which sends the hip-attacking Brailack tumbling away. With a kick that would dent hull plating, Gabe sends his small nemesis sailing through the compartment to smack against the far bulkhead, making a wet-sounding noise.

"Gabe, you there buddy?"

Gabe looks up at the ceiling, and as the final Brailack moves to his back, out of reach of both arms, he straightens and falls backward, crushing the small alien underneath him. It makes a gurgling noise as the droid rolls over, stands and walks to the control panel on the workbench. "Engineering is secure, Captain." Gabe looks down at his arm, still erupting in sparks. "Three hostiles, no longer a concern."

"Good job! Get the computer back under control and get the wireless network back up and running so we can use our wrist-comms. I'm pretty sure we're flying blind."

"Right away."

"WHAT THE WURRIN IS GOING ON OVER THERE?"

Xarrix and Jurrella are looking at the massive display at the front of the *Berserker's* bridge. The warlord turns to Xarrix, her face making it clear she expects an answer.

"I believe I had told you that Wil and the crew of the *Ghost* were... how did I put it, wild cards." He shrugs. "I'm sure it's fine. Lorath is over there, and I've seen her lead teams to pacify entire villages and not blink. The crew of the *Ghost* will not be a problem."

"Then why are they flying out of the engagement area? They're on a direct course towards," and Jurrella leans over the shoulder of one of her crew, looking at the hapless crew member's display, "... nowhere. They're flying at almost full sub-light speed to nowhere in particular."

Xarrix snaps his fingers at one of the crew at a station a few meters away. "You there, keep trying to hail the *Ghost*."

After glancing at the Duchess, the crew member nods. "Of course, sir."

Xarrix comes back over and bows slightly. "I'm sure everything is under control over there. Lorath is my top operative, remember."

The Duchess looks Xarrix up and down. "It had better be. We aren't done here, and I'm not convinced that there won't be more attacks!"

OPERATION: TAKE BACK THE SHIP. PHASE 4

Inside a cavity—because 'room' doesn't quite cut it as a description—that's at least thirty meters in each direction, the two women are standing over several bodies.

"Did you have to kill to them all?" Zephyr kicks one of the salvagers' bodies.

"Former assassin, remember." The feline-featured killer smiles. "Plus, we didn't need them for anything, did we?"

Leaning down to search the body, Zephyr says, "Besides information, no." She pats a few pocks. "Anything on that one?"

"Nope. Wait." Cynthia unzips the jumpsuit the four-legged alien is wearing, reaching down inside the lower half.

"Really?"

Cynthia tuts, as she reaches inside and withdraws a data card. She turns to Zephyr and winks, then inserts the card in the slot on her wristcomm. She looks at it for a moment, then looks up and turns her head this way and that before settling on something at the far end of the space they're in. Pointing, she says, "That's it."

The space they are in is roughly square shaped. There isn't a hard angle anywhere, and there are several ridges and protrusions fanning out from a something that's near the far wall, where the bow of the ship-creature would be. The salvagers have set up basic consoles around the room: navigation, flight controls, comms.

"You're sure?" Zephyr starts toward the oddly shaped mass; it's ridged and pulses slightly with a rhythm similar to breathing. There are massive organic-looking conduits connected to the structure. Several are severed or in a state of being severed, the wiring for the consoles spliced into them.

"Not even remotely, but that guy's data card says that that is the brain—or at least part of it."

Shrugging, Zephyr walks up to the large mass. It smells a little like grum; malty and earthy at the same time. "Wil would be retching right now," she says as she reaches out to touch it.

"Is that a—" Cynthia starts, then Zephyr can't hear her. Her vision swims, and then everything is black.

PLEASE.

  "Please, what?"

  Stop.

  "I don't understand. Are you in my head? Am I in yours? Well, I guess technically I—"

  Pain.

  "We're not with those that were harming you. They can't hurt you now. What are you?"

  Gomtu.

  "Is that your name or your species?"

  I am Gomtu, we are The Children.

  "Do you know where you are? What's been happening to the others?"

  Dead, but not dead.

  "Yes, many of them are. Those we came with are harming them."

  Why?

  "I'm afraid your species has a unique quality. Your bodies are essentially starships. Those others want to use you as cargo vessels and ships of war."

War? No.

CYNTHIA'S WRISTCOMM CRACKLES WITH STATIC THEN GOES SILENT. She looks down, waiting for it to do something more. When it doesn't, she lifts her arm. "Uh, Wil?" She is standing next to the seemingly inert Zephyr, who's standing ramrod straight, hand resting on the slowly pulsing mass.

The wrist comm crackles again. "Go ahead? You guys okay?"

"Sort of, something is happening with Zephyr, she—"

"What happened?" Maxim cuts in.

"She touched what we think is the brain of the Behemoth we're aboard. She hasn't moved since, and her lips are moving... like she's talking, or mumbling to someone."

"We're working on getting the *Ghost* back under control, but at the moment you're on your own. We're under thrust, flying blind, comms just came back," Wil says.

"Seems dangerous."

"Very." The strain is evident in his voice.

"Then I'll figure it out. Get back here, fast. Be careful though, don't forget Follux Sul is out there. Xarrix may not open fire on you with Lorath aboard, but I wouldn't stake my life on that."

"Uh, yeah, that's kind of moot anyhow," Wil's voice trails off. "Stay safe, we'll be back as soon as humanly possible."

"That's a low bar," the Tygran says, tapping the wristcomm to close the connection. She looks around the room—big brain like thing, Zephyr, a bunch of dead aliens and heavy equipment. Shrugging, she walks over the nearest body. "Inventory time, I guess."

WE DO NOT WANT TO FIGHT.

"No one does. Why are you all here? Why are you drifting dormant?"

Hibernation. My kind spend... thousands of cycles roaming the galaxy, but then must spend time in a state of hibernation. It replenishes us.

"It made you targets, this time."

Help us.

"How?"

Wake the others.

PART FOUR

CHAPTER XV

OH, IT'S ON!

After dragging the bodies to the cargo hold, the remaining crew of the *Ghost* are back on the bridge. "Captain, I have regained control of the ship," Gabe reports over the ship's comms. "All primary systems are now under our control, though many are not functioning at peak performance."

Wil looks at his station. The red blinking indicators from before are now a happier, less blinky, green, while a few are still yellow. The display that shows a tactical view of nearby space is online again and showing the *Ghost* hurtling off into nothing. He grabs the controls. "Great work, buddy." He brings the ship hard around back toward the salvage operation. "We're going to need weapons and shields, you got that?"

"Weapons are available now. I believe I can have shields online by the time we reach the engagement area."

Wil glances at Maxim, who shrugs. "Anything we can do to help?" he asks.

"No." The comms system beeps, closing the channel.

"He still in a bad mood over the whole bot-torture thing the other day?" Bennie asks.

"Dude, could you be more insensitive?" Wil glowers at the Brailack hacker.

"I could try."

Wil shakes his head. "Sometimes I wonder what's wrong with you."

Bennie shrugs. "The ladies don't seem to mind."

Maxim makes a retching noise, but Wil laughs. "I needed that. Alright, we'll be back in the engagement area in," he looks down at a display to his right, then looks to his left, "fifteen centocks." He begins adjusting the console to his preferred arrangement, muttering about Lorath touching his stuff.

Maxim looks down at his own display. "Enough time for a level two diagnostic, and to get my station re-configured. That stupid Sylban changed everything."

"Yeah, Lorath did a number on my station too. They were on the bridge what? half a day?"

"Mine is fine," Bennie offers, running his little green hand along the edge of the station. When he comes across something sticky he picks at it briefly.

"That's because it's disgusting, and even gangsters and mercenaries have cleanliness standards," Maxim offers.

Bennie flips Maxim off, then turns to Wil. "So what're we gonna do?" He gestures vaguely toward the direction of the cargo hold. "We've got a hold full of bodies, and Follux Sul is still out there. His ship is easily a match for us, and then some."

"Hey!" Wil snaps.

"What? I don't want to die," Bennie says, spreading his hands.

"We nearly die all the time. We almost died just a few months ago aboard the *Siege Perilous*."

"Uh, yeah. I was aboard the *Ghost* when those mechanical nightmares ripped their way into the ship. It wasn't fun, or something I want to do again, especially so soon." Bennie is a slightly paler green now, remembering.

Wil gets up and crosses to his diminutive friend. "Hey, we always survive." He pats Bennie's shoulder.

"We've literally only been together, what, barely two cycles?"

"Feels longer," Maxim offers.

"Plus, Gabe technically died on that monster dreadnaught," Bennie points out.

Wil forces a smile. "Well yeah, but he got better."

Bennie sighs and shoves Wil away.

"AH!" ZEPHYR EXHALES LOUDLY, HER HAND FALLING TO HER SIDE. Cynthia rushes to catch her as she collapses, easing her to the deck.

"What happened?"

"Water?" the pale ex-Peacekeeper croaks.

Cynthia looks around. "Oh, uh, yeah. Hold on." She lowers Zephyr to a sitting position, then rushes over to a small table the salvagers had set up with snacks and bottles of water. Handing Zephyr a bottle she asks, "What was that? What happened? You've been out for almost half a tock."

Zephyr shakes her head slowly, then takes a long sip of the water. "They're sentient." She gestures the space they're in, the brain structure nearby. "They feel pain, sadness—so much sadness."

"Grolack," Cynthia mutters. "Xarrix swore they were nothing more than beasts of burden at best. What do we do now?"

"It's already done," Zephyr says, handing the water to Cynthia and attempting to stand. "We need to go. Gomtu and the others aren't going to wait."

"Gum toe?" Cynthia hands Zephyr the water back when she's fully upright.

"Gomtu. That's this creatures' name. They name themselves when they reach maturity. This is a herd, a family unit. They have to hibernate every few thousand cycles for a few hundred cycles to replenish themselves. They absorb radiation from space." She starts her way to the opening they came from, waving her companion to follow. "Let's go."

"Go where? We jettisoned the salvager ship we came in through," Cynthia reminds her, walking as fast as she can to keep up with the now-energized Zephyr. "One of the other ships?"

"Gomtu is or will be forcing those ships off of him. Airlock, Wil can pick us up."

"Oh, wonderful. Just us and our musty second-hand space suits surrounded by pissed off living starships," Cynthia quips.

STAMPEDE!

As the *Ghost* approaches the engagement area, a space roughly a few million kilometers in radius where the Behemoths had been sleeping, Wil looks at the tactical display. "Uh, what the hell is going on?" He nods toward the smaller display next to the main screen, which is showing a lot of unidentified yellow, triangles moving erratically around the screen.

"Oh man, you said there wasn't going to be another fleet battle," Bennie whines. "I hate fleet battles!"

"Dude, where would a fleet even come from? Werdlow Three doesn't have one, that's why we're here. No one else knows what's going on or would even care." Wil looks up. "Computer, open channel to Zephyr." When the telltale beep is heard, he calls, "Hey ladies! We're back, where are you?"

The comms crackle with static. Zephyr's voice answers: "We're EVA. Gomtu and the others are stampeding."

"Gomtu?" Maxim asks.

"Stampeding?" Wil asks.

"Long story, and one I'd rather tell from the safety of, you know, inside the ship." A light on Wil's controls blinks on. "I've activated my beacon. Hurry up—these suits weren't meant to keep someone alive EVA this long."

"And they smell!" Cynthia hisses.

"I see it, heading your way now." Wil works the controls, moving the *Ghost* smoothly onto a course that will intercept Zephyr's beacon. "Uh, you know you're right in the middle of the stampede, right?"

"Gomtu is having the others keep us safe. I think they'll make a path for you."

"You think?"

"Well, it wasn't exactly an easy conversation. I think I was able to express to him that the *Ghost* is a friend." The comms burst into static. "—that or he thinks the *Butcher* is friendly and you're not. I'm not really sure."

"Lovely," Wil says, bringing the *Ghost* under one of the now very-active Behemoths, narrowly avoiding it as it turns slightly toward the *Ghost*. Another of the living vessels makes an abrupt turn toward them, almost colliding with one of its own, while attempting to squish the smaller Ankarran craft between them. "Yeah, I think we know the answer to who they think is friendly. Two centocks out."

"I'll go man the cargo doors. Scoop and move?" Maxim is heading for the hatch leading off the bridge.

"Almost certainly," Wil says without even looking at his big friend, his eyes not leaving his controls. "Bennie, sensors."

"On it," the small alien hacker replies, then, "Slaved to my station. Dren."

"Dren?" Wil asks as the hatch to the bridge closes behind Maxim.

"The *Butcher* is making its way towards us, opposite side of the melee of monsters. The *Berserker* is too. The Behemoths seem to be making a path for the *Butcher*."

"Of course they are. Okay, priorities—keep me posted on the *Butcher*, the *Berserker* is too slow to be an immediate threat. Plus, Gum shoe and his, her, its buddies think the battleship isn't friendly, so they'll do their part." He glances at the tactical display. "I hope."

"I see them!" Bennie points to the main display. There's a green circle on it—Zephyr and Cynthia, too small to see with the naked eye, are in the center of it.

"Me too, here we go." Wil adjusts his controls, then looks at the ceiling. "Get ready Max."

"Ready down here."

"*Butcher* is three centocks out and closing. They're almost full sub-light. Firing on any of the behemoths that get in their way," Bennie reports, tension making his ordinarily high-pitched voice just that much higher.

"Hopefully the big ship-shaped aliens will catch on that he's the baddie, and not us," Wil says, slowing the *Ghost* enough so that the women he's about to scoop up won't slam into the back of the cargo hold at thousands of meters per second.

"Got them!" Maxim shouts over the comms.

"Bennie, you may need to take weapons for a minute!" Wil says, pushing the sub-light engine throttle all the way forward.

"On it! I'll light 'em up!"

"I'll settle for enough erratic fire to keep them off balance," Wil says, swinging the ship wide, luring one of the smaller behemoths into a chase. "Guess junior hasn't figured out who the good guys are yet."

"Incoming comms," Bennie says before pressing a button his station, causing the telltale beep to come from the overhead speakers.

"It will be enjoyable to destroy you," Follux Sul says.

Wil reaches for a control. "Fuck off, munchkin." He presses the control, and the comms close.

"You said 'munchkin' was a term of endearment!" Bennie shouts.

NOT IN KANSAS ANYMORE

The *Ghost* rocks violently as the bridge hatch opens. Zephyr, Cynthia and Maxim lurch in, holding on to anything they can to keep from tumbling.

"About time! I've been doing all your jobs—well except you Cynthia, you don't have a job," Bennie says. He slaps several controls on one of his consoles, releasing tactical and sensors back to Maxim and Zephyr's stations, which come back to life immediately.

Cynthia bares her teeth, causing Bennie to turn back to his station. "What can I do?" The ship bucks and sparks erupt from a junction box next to the hatch, so she moves to quickly extinguish the small flame that has flared up.

"Can you get on the horn to you and Zee's new friends? It'd be awesome if they'd help some, or at least stop trying to crush us." Wil pushes hard on the flight controls. "Gotcha!"

On the tactical display, the icon of the *Ghost* with a smaller Behemoth right behind it swings around one of the largest living ships before turning hard to port. The young Behemoth, unable to adjust as quickly, continues on, right into the flight path of the *Butcher*. Unfortunately for the probably juvenile Behemoth it gets blasted to pieces by the *Butcher*, as it dodges around the now wreckage.

Wil wipes sweat from his forehead. "It's like fighting in the middle of a herd of brontosaurus; dodging weapons fire and trying to not get stepped on!"

"Nicely done," Maxim says, before letting loose two missiles that immediately hang tight U-turns in front of the ship and streak behind it towards the still off balance newer-model Ankarran ship. "What's a brontosaur?"

"Zephyr, I think it'll only speak to you?" Cynthia says, one hand to her ear, where she's made use of the comm station headgear. "It just keeps replying 'not you,' every time I make contact. None of the others seem to be interested in replying at all—or capable, I'm not sure which."

"Swap!" Zephyr says, standing and rushing over to the station Cynthia is occupying. "Keep an eye on the sensors."

The feline woman makes a similar dash to the other station. "On it."

Wil can hear Zephyr speaking into the headset.

"Swing to the starboard!" Cynthia shouts.

Without questioning the order, Wil does as she says, just as two smaller Behemoths collide. Had he not moved, the *Ghost* would have been right between them. He turns and nods once to her. The two smaller creatures separate, their skin ruptured, venting gasses but otherwise none the worse for the impact.

"Uh, the *Berserker* is moving off," Cynthia warns.

"What?" Wil says, glancing at the tactical display. "Oh shit, bet they didn't expect that." On the screen, a dozen or more of the massive space-dwelling living starships are ramming the gigantic battleship. Three of the beasts are drifting away. Wil isn't sure if they're dead or just injured—they're venting gasses and various other substances, large holes riddling their sides. The massive battle-ship, while slow, is not lacking in guns and is cutting the attacking Behemoths down at an alarming rate.

"The *Butcher* is turning tail!" Cynthia shouts.

"What the hell—"

"They're moving into position with the captured ships, looks like a defensive position," the Tygran woman reports.

Zephyr looks at Wil. "Sorry, that took a long time. For what it's worth, they see the *Ghost* as a friend now."

"Better late than never, I guess," Wil says.

"There's more." She listens intently. "They'd like us to accompany them to the place of forever—their term."

"Where is that?" Maxim asks.

"Now?" Wil asks.

Zephyr shrugs. Standing up, she nods to Cynthia. The two women quickly switch stations again.

"Uh, I think we're about to find out." Bennie points to the main screen. On it, the Behemoths are nudging their dead and injured into position around the *Ghost*. The healthiest of them move to form a loose sphere around the *Ghost* and the fallen Behemoths.

"What're they doing?" Wil asks, looking at Cynthia.

The Tygran woman shrugs. "Ask the ship whisperer."

But Zephyr shrugs too. "No idea. Talked to one of them, not an expert." She turns to look back at the main screen.

Maxim gestures to the screen. "To echo Bennie, I think we're about to find out." The Behemoths, the healthier ones at least, are all glowing. Lines all along their hulls are lighting up like blue lightning. Ahead of the impromptu fleet, the stars begin to distort—and with a flash, they're clearly somewhere else.

A wave of nausea washes over Wil. "The hell—"

"Working on getting a fix on our location," Zephyr says, one hand raised to her mouth, her color slightly off.

Wil looks at Maxim. "Threat board?"

"Clear. It's just us and the Behemoths."

"Not sure that counts as safe, just yet," Wil replies. Maxim shrugs.

Zephyr looks at Wil. "Um, we're nearly two thousand light years from where we just were."

"No way." Wil gets up and walks to her station. Looking over her shoulder, he swears. "Holy crap. Can you hail your pal gumshoe?"

"Gomtu," Zephyr corrects. As Wil moves back to his station, she announces, "Well, we're all invited aboard Gomtu to," she mimics an air quotes gesture she's seen Wil make, "witness the passing of their kin to the next realm."

"Oh good, funerals. Those're fun," Wil sighs.

WEIRDER AND WEIRDER

"Is this..." Wil starts.

"His brain? Yeah, essentially," Zephyr says, as the crew of the *Ghost* enters the same chamber that Zephyr and Cynthia found earlier. "Though it's in better shape than when we were last here." She looks around: the bodies of the salvagers are gone, as are the temporary bridge control consoles that were being wired into Gomtu's core functions. The damage to the conduits around the room seems to have been repaired. Out of the corner of her eye, she spots three little yellow lights. "Guys," she points.

"Great, tiny monsters, living inside huge ones," Wil says, resting his hand on his pulse pistol.

A small being comes out of the shadows. The three yellow lights are its eyes. It's barely half a meter tall, bipedal, and metallic looking, with a greenish tint to its outer casing.

"Droid of some type?" Maxim asks.

"I am an avatar," it says. It's voice deeper than Maxim's. "I have been assembled to interact with you." It gestures with a hand that looks just like a Palorian's—three fingers, two thumbs. "Gomtu is pleased you've come."

Bennie walks over and taps the avatars' head. "It's metal."

"My outer casing is the same material as Gomtu's outer hull," the avatar replies.

"Neat," Bennie says. "Can we keep it?"

Wil sighs, ignoring his rude little friend. "So what, we can speak to Gomtu through you? Like an interpreter?"

The small construct nods. "After a fashion. A more accurate interpretation would be that I am Gomtu. He can hear and understand everything you say, anywhere aboard. Speaking to you, however, is much more difficult," the avatar gestures to Zephyr, "as Zephyr discovered."

The Palorian woman shudders. "Yeah, I don't think I want to do that again. No offense, Gomtu," she adds, looking at the ceiling with a smile. The lighting in the room dims then returns to normal.

The avatar nods. "Gomtu feels the same. While it was beneficial at the time, it is taxing for the Children to merge minds like that with lesser beings. Hence the reason for my assembly."

"The children?" Gabe asks.

"Lesser?" Cynthia chuckles, looking at Zephyr.

"Assembled?" asks Bennie.

Zephyr flips Cynthia off, then turns to Gabe. "That's what they call themselves, the Children of the Expanse. They don't have any real concept of species or race."

The small avatar nods, then turns toward a portion of the bulkhead that is blank—then abruptly isn't. A display screen three times larger than that of the *Ghost* comes to life. On it dozens of the surviving "Children" have nudged their dead into formation, sending them drifting deeper into the nebula. "This is the place of forever, where the children bring their dead.

"No matter where the Children travel, when one of theirs dies, it is brought here to where their life started."

"Can the damaged ones be saved?" Wil asks, turning to look at the small avatar.

"They are being evaluated now. Normally, the answer would be yes in all cases; the Children are incredibly resilient. However, their rest cycle was interrupted, and none among them are at full power. If they were at full power, they could lend their energies to those in need." It spreads its tiny hands expansively. "It is unlikely the more gravely wounded will survive, there is simply not enough energy among the unharmed to share."

Gabe has been standing near the structure Zephyr indicated as Gomtu's brain. He turns now to the avatar. "You said this place is where the Children were born. Were they constructed? Is there a facility somewhere in this nebula?"

The avatar shakes its head. "Yes, and no. Several millennia ago, the first Children awoke," it gestures to the screen, "here. They had no idea what they were, or what their purpose was. They simply were. For hundreds of cycles they stayed here; mating, growing their numbers, observing. Eventually, their curiosity got to be too powerful. They ventured beyond the nebular gasses when their numbers were such that they felt safe in leaving the place of their creation."

"Cool," Bennie says in a hushed voice, watching the screen. The dead are being nudged deeper into the nebula, their bodies already beginning to fade and dissolve as they drift into the deeper regions.

"Further inside the nebula, there are elements that cause the bodies of the dead to dissolve back into the nebular material, replenishing it," the avatar explains. "When new Children are born, those who have perished will help construct the new."

"Um, so, for thousands of years, these guys just wander around deep space, like a pod of giant space sperm whales, then eventually get tired and take a long-ass nap?" Wil asks.

The avatar tilts its head to one side and stairs at Wil, its three eyes unblinking. "No. Well, not entirely."

Wil looks at Zephyr, who shrugs.

"The Children encountered a race called the Tendine. They were a kind race, deeply curious. They had limited space travel of their own when the Children entered their solar system. The Children, also curious, studied the worlds of the Tendine star system, until the two were able to communicate with each other." The avatar pauses. "It did not take long for the Children and Tendine to realize they shared a deep mutual love of exploration. The two species became partners, for the Tendine had limited means of leaving their solar system—their world was not rich in certain minerals and ores necessary for more advanced alloys. In exchange for passage aboard the Children, they offered themselves as custodians and caregivers to help make internal repairs and keep the Children healthy. Even though each Child creates small helper units, having living beings aboard was rewarding." The small construct rests a hand on its chest. "I am modeled after the Tendine. Each Child took as many Tendine as possible aboard, and the herd resumed its slow exploration of the cosmos."

Bennie, who has now become very interested in the story and has turned his full attention to the avatar, asks, "So what happened? To the Tendine, I mean. They're clearly not here, are they aboard other Children? Did they go back home?"

The avatar gives a sad shake of its head. "The Tendine fell to a virus they encountered on a world nearly five thousand light years from here. They worked tirelessly to find a cure, visiting thousands of worlds and species, but were ultimately unsuccessful. The last Tendine passed over one thousand cycles ago."

"I'm so sorry Gomtu," Zephyr says, resting her hand on the bulkhead.

The lights in the room dim briefly.

Wil looks around, then offers, "I may have a way to help the injured Children."

CHAPTER XVI

NO ONE LIKES SECRETS

"Are you grolacking insane?" Zephyr asks. She's pacing the mostly empty cargo hold, fuming.

"You could be so rich!" Cynthia observes. "Oh, and Xarrix is going to be pissed if he ever finds out. How did he not kill you for losing them?"

Wil shrugs. "Well I might have implied that they were never in the crate. I heard he maybe killed the guy I picked the crate up from." When Gabe turns to look at him, he adds, defensively, "The dude was a smuggler, and I heard he trafficked in kids sometimes."

Gabe says nothing, turning back to look at the smuggler's hold, which is now open. "I am impressed, I was not familiar with this compartment," he says, leaning to peer inside.

"I purged all records from the main computer when I had it installed. Hardly use it, to be honest." Wil gestures to the crystals at the bottom of the space. "These were under my bed until a few days ago, when we got stopped by that Peacekeeper corvette in the Brai system."

"Seems safe," Maxim says. "Hope you didn't want to have children."

Wil blanches. "Wait, what? Nothing I read said anything—" He spots the grin on his big Palorian friends' face. "Asshole." He leans down and hops into the small compartment. "They're charged, as far as I know, and we can charge any that aren't from the *Ghost*'s reactor."

"That's why you were acting so weird?" Zephyr asks.

"You got this ship shot to pieces over Harrith, then fought that giant dreadnaught, with charged Trillorium under your bed?" Cynthia asks. She turns, mumbling something about being either brave or stupid.

The small green avatar has been examining the contents of the hold. "These crystals contain tremendous amounts of energy. Your Captain is correct, they could be used to restore some of the injured Children."

Wil looks at Gabe. "Can you and Kermit inventory these and figure out who needs how many? Work out a distribution plan."

Gabe nods. "Of course, Captain." He gestures to the avatar, who comes over to sit at the edge of the hold.

WITH GABE AND THE AVATAR BACK ABOARD GOMTU, DISCUSSING THE distribution of the Trillorium with the other Children, the rest of the crew assembles in the lounge.

"I can't believe you kept something like this from us." Zephyr is still mad. "For one thing, those things could have exploded at any time, especially just rattling around under your bed." She looks at Wil, who is sitting across from her at the small kitchen table. "How did the Ankarrans or the Harrith not find them?"

"Or Bennie for that matter? He's always in your quarters snooping around," Maxim says.

Wil shrugs. "I assume neither group went into my quarters. In fact, if I recall they didn't have to go in any of our rooms, right? Plus, the crates are shielded against all but a really focused scan, and who would scan my bed?"

"No one that wants to keep their lunch down," Maxim says, as he grabs a handful of little pouches from the cupboard, tossing one to each member of the crew.

Wil adds, "I only moved them because of that Peacekeeper patrol back in the Brai system."

Zephyr is thinking now. "You're right, the lounge and crew berths were still intact—and from what I recall they didn't need access to them, beyond running some new wire and conduit through here." She glares at Wil. "Talk about lucking out."

Bennie takes a bite of the meal bar he's unwrapped. "Gross, bloo-berry. Trade me." He thrusts his energy bar across the table at Wil, who sighs and trades his mint-chocolate-chip bar.

Cynthia is sitting off to one side, on the large lounge chair in the entertainment area. "I still can't believe you didn't sell those. You could be living on an island on a beautiful water planet with the proceeds." She looks at Wil seriously. "Xarrix is going to be *pissed*," she says again.

Wil tuts. "I'd get bored. Besides, those are worse than blood diamonds, there's no way I could put them in circulation. Plus, screw Xarrix for one thing. And for another, I think the whole *I killed Lorath* thing might be more pressing to him."

"You don't know him at all." She shakes her head, then frowns. "What's a blood diamond?"

"On Earth—back in the day, before we got really good with synthetic diamonds—we had to mine them. Their rarity made them worth a fortune. Some of the biggest mines were in war-torn parts of the world. They were mined with slave labor, and the profits kept the warlords in business." He glances down, then back to Cynthia. "Almost the entire world got together and said, no more, they wouldn't buy blood diamonds, and after that any diamond that couldn't prove its place of origin was assumed to be a blood diamond. It took years to break the back of the warlords and cartels, but in the meantime, science figured out how to make a flawless arti-ficial diamond—so on top of the resistance to blood diamonds, the overall diamond market tanked." He chuckles. "Diamonds went from a status symbol to lining decorative pots."

"I see," Cynthia says. "I see where you get it."

"Get what?" Wil asks.

"That nobility that Xarrix hates." She smiles.

Zephyr makes a choking noise, then sits up straighter. "So, what now? We distribute the Trillorium to the wounded, and then?"

Wil looks at his first officer. "Well, I'm hoping the Children will then return us to our neck of the woods. We're not stocked to fly two thousand light years home."

"Only Gabe would be around to see us get there," Bennie says. "Unless you're hiding stasis pods from us too?"

"Look, I apologized already. What else can I say?"

Zephyr sighs. "Just don't let it happen again. We're crew, we're family," she gestures to Bennie, "even him. No more secrets."

Wil nods. "Agreed."

Bennie leans over and whispers, "You don't have any right? Stasis pods? They're worth a fortune in certain markets."

THAT'S A HORRIBLE PLAN

It takes just over a week to distribute the Trillorium to the injured Children. Despite everything, many are still nervous about the small, well-armed ship in their midst.

The avatar had quickly prioritized which Children would get how much of the precious mineral, and with Gabe's help created a schedule to deliver and install it. Wil has tried not to think about how that decision was made, busying himself with repairs to the *Ghost*. Gabe oversaw hooking the crystals into the power systems of the Children. To a creature, they all seem to like the engineering bot.

When the work is done, Wil goes to find the avatar. It has been staying in the cargo hold when aboard the *Ghost*, so he sits on the edge of the smugglers hold, feet knocking against the wall of the hidden space. "So, um, now that the herd is healthy and everything, we'd like to get back to our part of the galaxy. No telling what Xarrix and Jurrella have been up to all this time we've been gone."

The small construct nods. "Of course, Captain Calder. The Children are also ready to depart." The avatar approaches Wil. "It is time to free those who have been abducted."

"Um, I don't know that they can be saved, little guy. As far as we know, their higher functions were severed. They've been lobotomized. Can that be repaired or reversed?"

"Unfortunately, no. Perhaps my word choice was incorrect. The Children wish to free the souls of their kin, even if they cannot free their bodies. They will destroy them, and any aboard. It is the next best thing to bringing them back here, which is their primary goal."

Wil sighs. "I see. Well, this is getting a bit deep."

The avatar inclines its green metallic head. "I do not understand, there is no water nearby, nor has the floor of this hold lowered."

Wil laughs. "I like you. Come on, you can explain what has to happen to the others."

A FEW HOURS LATER, THE CREW CAN SEE MOVEMENT AMONG THE giant creatures on screen. "They're forming up," Zephyr announces.

"It is interesting that they are able to manipulate space-time in such a way," Gabe says, from just inside the hatch.

Wil spins his chair around. "Wanted to see it from here, huh?"

The bot inclines his head. "Indeed. The avatar was unable to explain the mechanics of the process to me. It seems that the Children do not have a solid understanding of the process beyond," he makes an air quotes gesture, "'It just works.'"

Spinning back around, Wil grins. "You guys are getting really good at that. Well, don't blink. If it's like last time, it'll just take a second." On the main screen, the Children have formed up around the *Ghost* in the same spherical formation. The blue lightning is creeping along the lines of the massive creatures. "And, away we go…" Wil says, as the nebula distorts, only to be replaced a moment later with stars. Wil looks over to Zephyr, trying his best to keep his meal bar down.

"We're back. Well, more or less," she amends, "We're about two light years from where we were when we left."

"I guess warping space and time isn't an exact science," Wil says, pushing the sub-light throttles forward. "Let's go visit some old friends." On the screen, the Children have modified their formation into a circle in front of the *Ghost*.

Spinning in her own seat to look at the others, Zephyr asks, "So, what exactly is the plan?"

"Kermit already explained," Wil says.

"No… the Avatar explained what the Children plan to do." She gestures to the bridge. "What are we going to do?"

Wil snaps his fingers. "Oh! What are," he puts both hands on his chest, "*we* going to do? We're going to find Xarrix and give him back his second in command, then kill him."

Zephyr tuts, again. "Oh, that it? This is almost as bad as your 'we'll just fly right into the battle of Harrith and broadcast our data packet' idea."

"Or the 'we'll fly to Borrolo and single-handedly stop a gargantuan warship from calling its friends' plan," Bennie adds.

Wil affects a stricken look. "Hey, both of those plans worked, more or less."

Maxim grunts. "Mostly less."

"In some cases, a lot less," Zephyr adds.

"Fine, fine. I assume one of you has a better idea?"

"Actually, yes," Maxim says, a smile spreading across his face. As Wil motions him to go on, he explains, "We make it rain."

"Rain?" Bennie asks.

"Yup." And the big Palorian starts to outline his plan.

When he is finished, Wil says, "Okay, I admit, that's a better plan. Let's get a hold of Kermit."

SOMEONE'S BEEN SELLING WEAPONS

I t takes some convincing, but eventually the Children agree to the plan—mostly because it could help them in their own efforts to free their captured kin, and because Gabe has been able to express how unlikely to succeed the original plan was.

"Okay, coming up on Werdlow Three. Looks like everyone is here." Wil toggles a control and the main display switches to a tactical view, showing the *Berserker* and *Butcher* in orbit around the planet, with the remaining salvager fleet in holding position at what looks like Lagrange Point One, the point between Werdlow Three and its first moon where gravity is balanced between the two. Werdlow Three has two moons, one is about the same size as Earth's while the other is half as big. The salvagers seem to be flitting between the captured Behemoths—Wil can't think of them as Children, given what has been done to them.

"Uh, problem," Zephyr says as she taps her console, updating the main display. Several dozen yellow icons highlight, then turn red. They're in a loose formation around the *Berserker*.

"Any idea if they've armed them yet?" Wil asks.

"We were only gone for a few days. How many could they have possibly armed?" Bennie wonders.

"Looks like we're about to find out," Maxim offers as several red icons start to break off from the rest of the pack, the *Berserker* and *Butcher* among them. The salvagers depart the flotilla of captured creatures, heading for the far side of Werdlow Three.

"We're being hailed," Cynthia reports. She has largely taken over managing of comms, leaving Zephyr free to man the sensors and ship's operations.

"Any guesses?" Wil asks, motioning over his shoulder for the feline-featured woman to open the channel.

The main screen changes to Xarrix and the Duchess Jurrella. "I had hoped after that stunt you pulled, you'd have been smarter than this," Xarrix says. "What do you hope to accomplish? You should have left this region and never looked back. You had your money."

"Oh, come on. For one thing, when have you ever known me to do the," Wil makes air quotes, "'reasonable thing'? For another, there's some unfinished business that needs settling. Like you not telling us that we'd be helping murder and enslave sentient beings."

"Which is it? Murder or enslave?" Xarrix asks mildly.

Wil makes a face. "Well, I mean, both really. Did you know they were sentient? That each of those vessels was really a giant space-faring, living creature? A creature with a name, and a sense of self? Did you know the salvagers where lobotomizing them to install bridge controls so that she," he jabs a finger at Jurrella, "could have people fly their bodies around?"

Xarrix makes a dismissive motion. "The Duchess and I went over the ins and outs of the situation, yes. After all, we had to brief the salvage teams."

"The ins and outs? Dude, its *murder*!" Wil leans forward in his chair. "She's building her fleet on the bodies of innocent creatures!"

"Oh, calm down, Human." The Duchess holds up a hand, silencing whatever Xarrix was about to say. "You were paid hand-somely, and despite your failure to complete your job, I'm not even going to demand that you return the funds."

"Wil," Maxim whispers. "They're accelerating, and the captured

Behemoths are moving to flank. They must have armed some of them. Sensors haven't been able to confirm yet."

Nodding, but otherwise not acknowledging his tactical officer, Wil continues, "How could you? I know you're a despicable gangster and all that, but this seems below you, Xarrix."

"Money is money, Wil. You of all people should know that. You've certainly done plenty of jobs for me that you found distasteful. I don't recall you ever returning a payment."

"I turned down plenty of jobs over the years, and I never enslaved living creatures!"

"Well, now you can add it to your resume. It'll make you eminently more hirable in certain circles," Jurrella offers, then glances offscreen. When she turns back to Wil, she's grinning.

Without a word, Wil slams the sub-light throttles to full speed and brings the *Ghost* around in a hard turn, right into the group of armed Behemoths attempting to flank them from the starboard side.

"Fire!" Jurrella shouts, then, "What do you mean...? Catch them!" The screen cuts back to the default forward view, which right now is showing a rapidly approaching Behemoth. A very heavily armed Behemoth.

"Max," Wil starts to say, but is interrupted by the sound of launching ordinance. "Nevermind."

On the screen the Behemoth they are charging directly toward is rocked by several explosions. "Booyah!" Maxim shouts, as the massive creature lists to the side, gasses venting from several tears in its hull, internal components streaming out the wound. What looks like a hastily mounted quad cannon is drifting away from the creature.

"Booyah?" Wil says, bringing the *Ghost* into another hard turn, this time in the opposite direction they'd been flying in a moment ago—just in time to dodge a smaller and faster Behemoth, outfitted as a frigate from the looks of it, with two missile launchers tracking the *Ghost*.

"I got it right, right?" the big man says, barely glancing at Wil as he works on targeting another ship.

"Guh! Yup, you got it right!" Wil says as the ship lurches to one side before he can correct. Sparks fall from an overloaded circuit somewhere overhead.

"Plasma blaster looks like an older model Peacekeeper version. Xarrix must have been stockpiling weapons for a while," Maxim reports, then highlights the offending creature on the tactical sub-display. "Looks like that one has four, two mounted on each side." The ship rocks again.

"Cynthia, can you—" Wil starts.

"Already done, they're on their way," she reports.

DEEP THOUGHTS AT WEIRD TIMES

"Where's the *Berserker*?" Wil asks, bringing the *Ghost* around on an attack run on one of the larger captured vessels.

"Well out of weapons range still," Zephyr says. "However…"

"This can't be good."

"The *Butcher* is accelerating." She looks over at Wil. "Towards us."

"Max, new focus—destroy the *Butcher*. We'll deal with Xarrix and Jurrella after that."

"Excellent!" the big Palorian says, focusing on his console.

"Cyn, hail Follux Sul," Wil orders, moving the *Ghost* down and around one of the armed Behemoths, whose weapons are firing wildly, mostly failing to connect with the nimble *Ghost*. "Zee, can you get a read on how many and which Behemoths are armed?"

"Here he is," Cynthia says.

"On it," Zephyr answers, just as the beep of the comms opening sounds.

"Ready to die, Captain good guy?" the diminutive space pirate asks.

"I mean overall, no, but I'm still relatively young. I think about my mortality more and more, though, you know—I guess just a part of getting older and stuff," Wil answers. "Maybe it's because I'm the only Human out here, fighting space scum like you, saving the GC from war and stuff. I've been taking supplements that, according to the doc I bought them from, should slow down the aging process."

"She wasn't a doctor," Bennie hisses.

Wil makes a strangled noise, then continues, "I dunno, I definitely think about death more now than I did before, you know?"

"What?" the Buttoxian pirate splutters, clearly confused.

"Oh, you meant, like today? Am I ready to die today?"

"Yes!"

"No, no I'm not. Plus, you know I'm the good guy here, we don't die easily. That said though, I hope you're ready to die!" He makes a slashing motion over his head, and Cynthia closes the channel. Pushing the controls forward, he brings the *Ghost* into a dive that takes the ship out of the battle briefly, luring the *Butcher* to follow.

Throughout the ship, several clanking sounds resonate. "Surprises away," Maxim reports.

"Hold on Gabe!" Wil shouts, glancing at the ceiling, as he pulls the controls back, pushing the throttles forward. He can hear the aft blasters firing. He toggles a control and the main display switches to a view aft. The newer-model Ankarran Raptor is gaining ground, its shields absorbing the blaster fire Maxim is dishing out, its own blasters raking the *Ghost's* shields in response. Suddenly, a few of the blaster bolts streaking from the *Ghost's* aft weapons aren't aimed at the *Butcher* anymore, but at the small scattered rocks drifting in space right in front of the ship—a few pieces of Trillorium Wil held back from the Children.

The blasts find their marks, striking each fist-sized crystal and freeing its stored energy charge. The space behind the *Ghost* and in front of and around the *Butcher* erupts in a massive discharge of energy. It pushes everyone aboard the *Ghost* back into their seats; the inertia dampers struggling to compensate. Wil can only guess what the crew of the *Butcher* is going through as the ship flies through a half dozen explosions that would rival a nuclear bomb. Maxim looks over to Wil. "Again, you had those under your bed?"

"In hindsight, it wasn't the best idea, I ad—"

"Bank starboard!" Zephyr interrupts. Wil does, just as a wave of blaster fire rakes the port edge of the *Ghost's* shields, causing alarms to go off throughout the bridge. "Behemoth coming in behind us!"

"I see it!" Wil pulls the controls hard over, trying to dodge the withering fire from the Behemoth, while not losing sight of the likely damaged *Butcher*. "Where's the *Butcher*? What's her status?" He shouts.

The ship rocks, and sparks erupt from an overloaded conduit above Bennie's station. Wil can hear the sound of the fore-and-aft weapons firing furiously at the target-rich environment. "The *Butcher*?"

"Found her—she's still under power, but her shields are nearly depleted." Zephyr reports. "I'm reading several overloaded emitters. Looks like her port nacelle is offline, no power to the engine or the disruptor array."

"Max, get ready." Wil looks over his shoulder. "See if our little pal will answer," he says to Cynthia.

"What is it you want, Human krebnack?" Follux Sul asks over the comms. His voice is hoarse, and in the background, Wil can hear coughing and the banging of tools on equipment. A klaxon is sounding somewhere on the enemy ship.

"Oh, nothing, just wanted to call and say goodbye," Wil says, his smile vicious.

"What? Where are... Where is he? Shields! Raise the—" Wil looks over at Maxim and nods.

"Captain Wil Calder!" the small pirate says quickly. "We can work something out! Our base has a warehouse full of stolen goods, worth millions of—" The sound of an explosion, followed by the rushing of air, is heard before the comm disconnects.

"We should try to find his warehouse—" Wil starts, when the *Ghost* is jolted violently, spinning the ship and sending everyone flying across the bridge. The sound of rending metal screeches through the ship.

"I knew this would happen!" Bennie screams.

FLIGHT OF THE VALKYRIES

"What the hell happened?" Wil asks, getting back to his feet. He's next to Bennie's station, having flown several feet from his command chair and pilot station.

"I think one of the captured behemoths rammed us," Zephyr replies.

"Captain, I can confirm Zephyr's hypothesis. I have accessed the sensor feeds to review, and one of the mid-sized creatures came out of nowhere and rammed us," Gabe says over the speakers. "I have taken over bridge control and moved the ship from the attacker; control is yours again."

"Nowhere?" Wil asks, then looks around the room. "You think they can do that teleporting thing individually? More importantly, you think Jurrella's salvage crews figured it out?" He makes it back to his chair, this time grabbing the five-point harness and fastening it.

Zephyr shrugs, as she helps Maxim up. He's bleeding from a severe-looking cut across his forehead and cradling one arm. The big Palorian looks up at Wil. "I'm still in the fight."

Wil shakes his head. "Sorry, big guy. Assuming we're in the fight at all, I need someone with two working arms on tactical." He looks at Zephyr, then at Cynthia, who is helping Bennie back into his seat. The Brailack looks shaken, one eye swollen shut. "Cynthia?"

She nods, and starts crossing the bridge. "I'm on it."

"Max, get down to medical, get the auto-doc to set your arm, then back up here as soon as you can." Looking at the ceiling, Wil calls, "Gabe, what's the deal? We still in this fight? Come to think of it, why hasn't teenage monster starship rammed us again?"

"The ship is heavily damaged, but I believe I can keep weapons and shields online. Propulsion was unharmed. Life support is marginal in some sections of the ship. The Behemoth that rammed us appears to be dazed, it is drifting in the opposite direction to the heading I have us on. I am reading several power surges along its bow and extensive structural damage."

"Make sure the med-bay is online, Max is on his way there with a broken arm," Wil says, taking his seat and resetting his controls. After a few sections of his panel flicker on and off, everything stabilizes. He looks at his console: the *Ghost* is tumble-flying haphazardly away from the fight. *Piloting isn't one of Gabe's strong suits, I guess,* Wil thinks, grasping the controls.

Zephyr works her console, and the main screen resets, showing a tactical view of the surrounding area. A mid-sized Behemoth—the same one that rammed them—is moving off to join the remaining red icons, slowly… which are all rushing towards a bunch of green icons. She whispers, "They're here."

Wil whistles. "Shit is about to get real." He looks at his console. "Hey Gabe, the port maneuvering thrusters are sticky, that something you can fix? Still gotta go up against the *Berserker*—would prefer to not do it only turning right."

"I will need a few minutes."

GABE LEAVES ENGINEERING AND HEADS FOR THE ACCESS CRAWLSPACE in the port wing. Last time he was in one of these confined spaces during a battle, the *Ghost* was over Harrith Prime. The access panel for the sticky maneuvering thruster is fused, he sees.

"Captain, I will have to go EVA to repair the port maneuvering thrusters. I am certain I can fix them. However, the main access panel in the wing is fused. Cutting through would take longer than the repair, and could cause unexpected damage."

Over the built-in comm in Gabe's head, Wil's voice replies: "That sounds dangerous. We're heading back towards the fight— Gomtu and the others are almost within weapons range of their kin, and they'll be deploying shortly."

"I am aware, but if you want to make left turns, this is the only option." Gabe is working his way back down the access chute, past many previous hasty repairs he's made to the ship in the last year.

"Okay, hurry," Wil says, the worry in his voice clear.

"Of course." Gabe wastes no time making his way to the small airlock set at the top of the *Ghost's* large aft section, just behind the ship's small med-bay. Accessing the ship's computer, he instructs the overheard doors to open. The maglocks in his feet de-activate and he fires his thrusters for a microtock, at ten percent power, just enough to push him out of the airlock and into space.

He turns left and walks down and around the hull, until he's on the port wing, looking at the faulty maneuvering thruster assembly. "I will need five centocks."

"You got it," Wil answers.

AS THE AUTO-DOC WORKS ON HIS ARM, MAXIM SEES GABE WALK past the entry towards the hatch to the top-side airlock. The auto-doc beeps, and Maxim withdraws his arm, rotating his hand a few times experimentally, and winces slightly. He grabs an emergency splint from a shelf on his way out.

CHAPTER XVII

JUMPING SHIP

On the *Ghost's* main display, the crew watches as Gomtu and the surviving children arrive in the Werdlow Three planetary system, each pushing an asteroid. To hide the asteroids from the enemy scanners, only the most massive Behemoths have one, hiding it in their enormous shadows.

"You know Wil, if this doesn't go as planned, we're killing thousands of people, most of whom have nothing to do with this," Zephyr says in a low voice, not taking her gaze from the screen. The Children are on a direct course for the enemy fleet, with the planet Werdlow Three directly behind them.

Wil nods. "Yeah, I do, but it's the only way to take Werdlow Three off the board. Jurrella can't have a fleet. She's too dangerous, just look at how effective the weaponized Behemoths are." He shakes his head. "Hell, look how effective the unarmed ones are. Alright, this isn't over, let's get back to it. Cyn, locate and keep a target lock on the *Berserker*."

"Done, I'm reading fluctuations in the port disruptor," she reports, then looks at the ceiling. "Gabe, can you take a look at the port disruptor while you're there? I'm getting weird power flow readings."

"Of course. Captain, you have maneuvering. Please, no sudden moves until I am back inside. The disruptor should take only a few centocks."

"Excellent! Thanks, buddy—and you got it, but hurry up. We'll be in weapons range of the *Berserker* in just a few minutes, tops."

On the screen, the Children have released their rocky payloads. It took some explaining, but each Child is equipped with some type of incredibly strong and prehensile docking cable. Using them to clutch the asteroids was Wil's idea. After dropping the *Ghost* off, the Children did their space-jump trick to get to the outer asteroid belt of the Werdlow system. Then they accelerated to their maximum sunlight speed, several fractions of the speed of light. The released asteroids are moving at thousands of meters a second on a direct course to the regrouping flotilla of captured Behemoths.

"Think Jurrella's people even saw them? The rocks, I mean," Cynthia asks, from the tactical station.

"Doubt it," Wil offers. "Those tow-cable things they used kept the rocks really close, and only the largest of them have rocks." He points. "The smaller ones are flying with the rocks, probably trying to hide them."

The first of the asteroids impact the captured Behemoths, smashing them to dust. The impacts are spectacular in their destructiveness; rings of released energy expand as behemoths shatter into millions of pieces, those aboard dying instantly, before they even have time to realize what is happening.

"Look!" Zephyr points, as several of the Children shimmer and vanish, only to appear behind the enemy fleet, deftly moving to capture stray asteroids that missed their intended targets. "I guess that answers that. Impressive—" she starts, then adds, "Oh no. Two got through."

On the screen, two of the Children are moving off, having missed their capture of the asteroids, which are now streaking through the atmosphere of Werdlow Three.

"No time to worry—" Wil starts.

"We're being targeted!" Zephyr shouts, breaking everyone out of their trances.

"Gabe hold on!" Wil shouts as he moves the *Ghost* out of range of the incoming energy weapons. "Gabe, get back in, done or not." There's no answer. "Gabe? Buddy?" Wil looks over at Zephyr, who is furiously scanning the area. Wil banks the ship again, dodging fire —the *Berserker*, slow as it is, has closed the gap. Wil hears the telltale whine of the forward disrupters firing, followed by the clank of missiles moving into position below.

"I have him!" Zephyr shouts. "Oh Grolack, he's on his way to the *Berserker*—with Maxim!" The fright in her voice is enough to make Wil look over at her.

"Bennie—" Wil starts.

"One second!" the Brailack says, then, "Okay I was able to override his comms lockout. You're on."

"What the ever-loving hell are you two doing?!" Wil demands.

"Sorry Captain, I was going to call in. I was getting patched up in the med-bay, and I saw Gabe head out. I suited up in case he needed help."

"What about your arm?" Wil asks.

"The auto-doc finished, and I grabbed an emergency splint. We were packing up when he just detached from the ship."

"He has flight capability, you don't," Zephyr growls.

"Well, yes, I didn't think that part through when I jumped after him, but thankfully Gabe came back to get me."

Gabe chimes in. "Captain, I am sorry, but I must put an end to the Duchess' treatment of droids."

"I thought killing her and Xarrix would accomplish that," Wil says, bringing the ship around in a tight arc, trying to draw as much fire as he can, while not getting hit. The latter is not working so well —sparks and small flames are erupting all over the bridge, and likely other parts of the ship.

"The destruction of the *Berserker* at the hands of the *Ghost*, as it were, is not a certainty," Gabe says, as calmly as if he was standing next to the bridge hatch.

"I don't fucking believe this! Gabe, is this the best time? The destruction of the *Berserker* is definitely impossible with you two dummies on it," Wil says, as the ship rattles, taking several point defense rounds at close range.

"Maxim, you idiot. This is foolhardy. Please..." Zephyr begs.

"My love, I couldn't let Gabe do this on his own." The sadness in the ex-Peacekeeper's voice makes it clear that he is unsure this isn't a one-way trip.

"Come back to me," she says in a low voice.

"Always," he replies. The *Ghost* rattles again, and something in the corridor explodes.

JUDGE AND JURY

"Okay, new plan," Wil says. "We help destroy her fleet, then we deal with the 'Duchess' and her ship." His sarcasm at the title is unmistakable. "Gabe, Max, you don't have long. The Children are fired up and smashing anything that isn't the *Ghost*. I don't know that they won't turn on the *Berserker* when that's all that's left, regardless of who's aboard," he warns.

The *Ghost* accelerates away from the massive warship, heading towards the very one-sided fight beyond. The asteroids have thinned the captured Behemoth's numbers, but there are still plenty remaining—at least half have weapons mounted on their hulls, ranging from blaster cannons and disruptors to missile batteries. Those with weapons are decimating their unarmed fellows.

"Fire everything we've got. If it isn't broadcasting the IFF signal we agreed on with the Children, blow it away," Wil says, glancing at Cynthia, her face lined with determination as she hunches over her console. The sound of the *Ghost's* weapons firing echoes through the ship.

THE AIRLOCK ON THE *BERSERKER* OPENS WITH A HISS. "THAT WAS surprisingly easy." Maxim observes, stepping out into the corridor.

"You doubted my sensors?" Gabe asks, stepping past his companion. Maxim says nothing. "This way," the bot says, heading off down the corridor.

"How do you know which way to go?" Maxim wonders.

"I gave the Captain a tracking device." When he sees Maxim's face, Gabe adds, "This was not the intended use, I assure you. I did not believe Xarrix or his client to be trustworthy and was worried that the Captain might be taken hostage or kidnapped to encourage the rest of us to comply." The engineering bot shrugs. "I figured it was a worthwhile strategy."

"That's pretty sound logic," Maxim admits. He looks over at the tall bot. "He's still going to be mad."

"Only if you tell him." Gabe glances down at Maxim, then increases his pace. "By analyzing the data from the tracker, the Captain spent most his time aboard this vessel in a large chamber near the center. I believe that to be the 'Throne Room,' as the Captain called it. The device had passive sensors that mapped the vessel as the captain moved through it."

"Wish I had a gun, or my armor... well, both really," Maxim complains, holding his splinted arm up to look at it, where the spacesuit material is stretched over the bulky device. The suit is one of the emergency suits, similar to those Zephyr and Cynthia had worn, and provides next to no protection from weapons fire. It also has no built-in weapons. "These smell, really bad."

"I did not ask you to come with me," Gabe points out.

"I know, but like I told Zephyr, you are crew, family, I know how upset you've been regarding that flobin's treatment of droids. Or I guess the treatment of droids in general, really."

"That is correct. Since my time aboard the *Siege Perilous* and being exposed to the existence of an entire civilization of machine intelligences, I have realized how truly horrible the treatment of cybernetic life forms within the GC is."

Maxim is silent for a beat. "Did any of this come up during your debrief with the Peacekeepers?"

"It did. We are here." Gabe stops at a massive hatchway. "My sensors indicate there are five beings on the other side."

Maxim holds both hands out. "No guns."

Gabe raises both arms, which transform into pulse blasters. "I have guns."

"Dren, yes you do." Maxim motions towards the door. "Lead the way."

Gabe lifts one leg and kicks the massive door, sending half of it flying inward, while the other half slouches to one side off its track. Without waiting for a reaction from inside, he levels his blasters and begins firing into the room as he enters. "The Peacekeepers did not seem overly interested in my thoughts on the treatment of droids and other sentient intelligences throughout the GC," he offers, as if they're sitting in the lounge on the *Ghost*.

Maxim ducks behind and follows him in. Under the part of the door that Gabe kicked is what looks like the remains of a body, what's left of an arm ending in a hand holding a pulse rifle. Maxim grabs the now ownerless weapon. "I'm armed. That's rather disgusting, they just ignored your concerns?"

"No need, and yes. The Senior Centurion assured me he would bring my report to his superiors. I do not believe he did."

Maxim looks up. In addition to whoever is under the remains of the door, three other guards are lying dead on the ground. "Despicable."

Jurrella is sitting on her throne, mashing the control panel.

"I have taken the liberty of jamming all network connections to this room," Gabe informs her. "Your network security measures are woefully inadequate. No help will be forthcoming."

"Where's Xarrix?" Maxim asks.

"You're here for him?" She grins. "By now that lowlife is boarding his ship, ready to depart. If you hurry, you can catch him."

Her sneer is infuriating. "I won't alert my warriors, if you leave now."

"I am not here for Xarrix. I am here for you, Duchess Jurrella of Werdlow Three. You torture droids for pleasure. You disregard the sentience of others." Gabe strides up to stand before the throne, his arms transforming back into their standard configuration. His eyes, however, are still their combat mode red.

"My what? My treatment of droids? Who cares about droids? I have my empire to worry about! Those creatures, tools, no different than droids!" She leans forward, not seeing the danger she's in. "My family built Werdlow Three from the nothing his kind," she levels a finger at Maxim, "left behind when they decided that my world wasn't worth their efforts or civilization." She sits upright. "When the noble Galactic Commonwealth fled the Werdlow system, they took their harvesters, their water purification factories, everything! I will lead my planet and my people into a glorious future of prosperity. If some droids are destroyed along the way, then so be it. If some nameless creatures have to live their lives serving Werdlow Three, so be it!"

"Uh, Gabe?" Maxim says. From down the corridor he can hear shouts.

"Cybernetic life forms are alive. Our makers build us that way. To better serve, you." Gabe's eyes glow a brighter red.

The would-be warlord sneers. "Yes, serve us. At our pleasure. We purchase you, your control keys ensure your obedience. We do with you what we want."

"You are horrible," Gabe says.

"Uh oh," Maxim murmurs as Gabe's left arm begins to whir and click, switching back into blaster mode. The metal of his forearm shifting to allow a twin-barreled blaster to lift out.

"On behalf of all cybernetic life, I do this. I will, one at a time, if needed, remove the most violent oppressors from this galaxy," the bot says, raising his arm.

"What? What are you—You can't harm me, your progra—"

The rest is lost in the sound of a single blaster bolt knocking her back against her throne, a smoldering hole left in her chest. Another shot ensures that Jurrella of Werdlow Three is well and truly dead, her dreams of empire building gone with her.

Gabe turns to Maxim, his eyes returning to non-combat-mode yellow. "We can go now." He smiles lopsidedly.

Maxim eyes his friend, as Gabe's weapons systems return to their standby locations in his forearms, "You know we could have taken her to the GC Supreme Court, they'd have tried her for this."

Gabe inclines his head, "My way, was more expedient."

The ship rocks and the lights dim for a moment. Wil's voice cuts in on the comms. "Guys, things are getting hairy out here, and the *Berserker* is wading into the middle of the battle. Probably a good idea to get out of there."

"Guess the Captain of this boat isn't waiting for orders from his Duchess," Maxim observes. He spins to face the destroyed main door, firing as two armed creatures—both the same species as Jurrella—enter, rifles drawn. Both fly back against the far wall of the corridor, smoking holes in their midsections. "Time to go."

Gabe nods. "Acknowledged Captain, we are almost ready. Be aware, Xarrix is or has already, fled the *Berserker*." Turning to Maxim, he says, "We should get to the launch bay." Without warning, a klaxon sounds. "With haste."

CLOSURE, I GUESS

"This ship is horribly designed," Maxim complains. Even with Gabe's enhanced sensors, they've had to double back twice when confronted with an inexplicable blockage in a corridor.

"Indeed, whoever built this vessel was either a genius or insane. I am unsure which, but likely the latter," Gabe replies guiding them through the maze of corridors, avoiding the massive battleship's crew whenever possible. "I am unfamiliar with the design. I should have asked Jurrella who the shipbuilder was."

"You know, killing her won't have—" The entire ship rumbles, the lights dim then return. "—any impact on droids rights, or even likely their treatment on Werdlow Three, or this ship, if it survives." Maxim ducks into a small maintenance closet behind Gabe. Two well-armed crew march past; one Hulgian, on Sylban.

The droid looks at his friend. "True. However, killing her will not have a negative impact on droids either. Plus, her own abuses of droids have now come to an end." He leads the way out of the maintenance closet that the two are hiding in. "We are almost there."

As they exit, the overhead speakers erupt. "They have killed The

Duchess! Intruders are aboard! Find them, kill them! Vengeance for the Duchess! Long live Werdlow Three!"

Maxim looks up. "Rather dramatic. We should hurry."

"THE CHILDREN ARE TAKING HEAVY LOSSES!" ZEPHYR REPORTS. "There are fewer than half the number that came back with us left!"

The *Ghost* narrowly dodges over the top of one of the smaller Children, bringing its guns to bear on one of the captured Behemoths—first destroying the single blaster cannon mounted on its dorsal section, then blowing several holes in it. Cynthia is nearly as good with the weapons as Maxim, rapidly dealing devastating blows on the enslaved beasts. *Where did Jurrella get enough people to crew all these ships?* he wonders. On the main screen, two of the larger Children are smashing a captured behemoth between their hulls.

The *Berserker* is right in the middle of the fray, firing on the Children while trying to fend off ramming attacks.

"Something just left the *Berserker*!" Zephyr says. "Looks like a small scout craft!"

"Heading?" Wil asks.

"Away from us." She looks over at Wil, the question clear on her face.

"Max? Gabe? What's going on? Is that you that just left the *Berserker*?"

"Negative, Captain. That must be Xarrix. We were too late to stop his departure," Gabe replies.

"Go after him, Wil!" Maxim shouts. "We'll be okay."

Wil looks at Zephyr, her face a mask of concern. She looks up and nods.

Wil pushes the ship hard over, following the fleeing vessel.

THE FLIGHT DECK OF THE MASSIVE *BERSERKER* IS DESERTED, NO doubt due to the ship being under-manned, having crewed every single captured Behemoth. The enormous hanger doors are still open after Xarrix's departure, and rows of shuttles stand ready for passengers off to the side of the ample space.

"Be careful over there!" Wil shouts, closing the channel.

"Affirmative. We need to get control of this ship, help the Children. Barring that, we need to destroy it." He looks at Gabe. "And ideally, not die in the process."

Gabe nods. "Agreed. I must access the main computer core. Help me find a terminal—someone has shut down the wireless network, no doubt hoping to hinder us. Someone on this ship is smarter than I gave them credit for."

Maxim looks around. "There!" He points. In the corner of the hangar is a ladder up to the flight control booth. Maxim rushes to the ladder, just as Gabe takes flight, lifting effortlessly up. "Show off," Maxim mumbles under his breath.

"HAIL THAT THING," WIL SAYS, AS THE *GHOST* CLOSES IN ON THE fleeing craft. It is clearly a modified scout vessel, as his sensors have identified several weapons emplacements. The battle of the Behemoths is millions of miles behind them already. The fleeing craft is almost clear of the gravity well of Werdlow Three—almost. Even damaged, the *Ghost* is able to close the distance between them.

The comms system beeps and the main display changes, showing Xarrix in the cockpit of the small vessel. "Well Human, you've cost me a fortune. Again."

"Icing on the cake," Wil says through gritted teeth. "It was one thing when you hired us to rob and kill other criminals to grow your empire. It's another thing entirely to willingly aide in the murder and enslavement of a sentient species. Not to mention standing by while that monster tortures droids."

"My, you've certainly gotten a thicker noble streak since finding your little band of misfits, haven't you?" He looks Wil in the eyes. "What is it you want? Return Lorath and her crew, and we can go about our lives, no retribution. I wouldn't frequent Fury though after this. Honestly I expected trouble from that diminutive psychopath Follux Sul, but I should have known better."

"Oh, I'm definitely planning on reuniting you with your henchwoman."

Xarrix looks over Wil's shoulder, to where he had become used to Cynthia sitting. "Got tired of the Tygran flobin already?"

From Maxim's station, Wil can hear Cynthia growling. The tactical station is just out of range of the video pickup.

"And you wonder why people don't like you," Wil sneers, casting a glance at the tactical sub-display. The *Ghost* is almost in weapons range. The fleeing ship drops several missiles behind it like mines, forcing Wil to maneuver around them. One explodes against the shields and the *Ghost* loses speed momentarily.

"What is it you want from me, Human? An apology? More money? Some type of ransom for Lorath?" The small craft turns abruptly, bringing its weapons to bear on the *Ghost*, raking the forward shields with blaster fire. Wil pushes the controls, dropping the *Ghost* below the oncoming fire. As the two ships pass, the *Ghost's* aft weapons stitch hot plasma across the lower shields of Xarrix's craft. On the screen, sparks shower the crime boss momentarily.

"Nice move. Speaking of Lorath, I'm sure she'd be touched you even considered paying a ransom," Wil says.

"Past tense? What have you done?" Xarrix is glaring now, his reptilian eyes narrowed to slits. The *Ghost* is back on a pursuit vector for the smaller craft. Xarrix is clearly pushing the engines beyond their tolerance range.

"Oh, Lorath is dead. Shot her myself. They're all dead, that crew you sent with her to take over my ship. Clever with that virus you planted, and the activation code in the payment data stick.

When did you do that? When you installed the stealth systems, or before that, when you made repairs?"

"Dead?" Xarrix seems taken aback.

"As a doornail. You'll be joining her soon. I'm not a religious person myself, but if there's an afterlife you can chat with her for the details, it's a good story. Well, not from her end—ends tragically and all that."

"I will kill you, Human. How dare you? After everything I've done for you?" Xarrix says, in a tone of voice Wil has never heard him use. "I swear to the gods you will wish Lanksham had never found you. You'll wish—"

"Bye, Xarrix. It's been fun knowing you—well, that's a lie, it's been pretty crappy knowing you. But at least you can die knowing you did one good thing; you brought this crew together." He nods once, knowing Cynthia is watching him and will know what he means. She does, and from deep inside the ship comes the tell-tale sound of the missile launch system cycling, then firing two missiles, then two more. As the rockets streak their way towards the fleeing craft, plasma blasts leave the forward weapons, striking the shields, depleting them enough for the missiles to do their jobs.

The small craft does it's best to destroy the incoming ordinance, taking out two of the inbound missiles, but not the final two.

"You'll regret this!" Xarrix shouts, frantically working the controls of his small craft, as sparks and smoke fills the screen, alongside more than one klaxon.

"I doubt it." Wil smiles now, as the screen dissolves into static. Xarrix screams, then the display switches to a view of the small expanding debris cloud that used to be one of the most powerful gangsters in the Galactic Commonwealth.

Wil turns a full circle, looking at his three remaining crew. "Let's go get our friends," he says.

CHAPTER XVIII

VIVA LA REVOLUCIÓN

"I have accessed the ship's systems," Gabe reports as Maxim climbs the last rungs of the ladder and enters the small control booth. "Isolating the bridge; accessing weapons and propulsion." Small glowing filaments have extruded from each of Gabe's fingers and snaked their way into the console he's standing at. Lights pulse up and down the length of the flexible protrusions.

Seeing the glowing filaments, Maxim says, "Those are new." He looks up at Gabe. "How is the *Ghost* doing? How are the Children doing?"

"The *Ghost* is pursuing Xarrix. Based on the current speed of both vessels, the Captain will catch Xarrix shortly before he is clear of the gravity well and able to go FTL." A pause as the bot accesses additional systems. "The Children have suffered tremendous losses. They've neutralized their un-weaponized kin—however, the armed variant are proving more than the Children can handle. If we do not intervene, they will wipe the Children out."

Gabe is silent for a time. Maxim is about to ask if he's alright, when he turns to the tall Palorian. "I have moved the ship further into the battle." As if to emphasize the point, the ship shakes. Somewhere nearby a section is torn open to space, if the sounds they can hear are any indicator. The lights flicker then return to normal. "This vessel is heavily damaged, but I am using the few remaining weapons to destroy as many captured behemoths as possible." He pauses. "I have also activated the self-destruct. And I have sealed the bridge and engineering sections and isolated them from accessing the ship's control systems. That should keep them busy."

"Man, you're kinda badass these days," Maxim observes. "Let's go, before the rest of the crew flood this compartment to evacuate."

"I have also sealed the doors to the launch deck." Smiling, Gabe lifts off the deck and flies himself down to the main deck of the shuttle bay.

"Show off!" Maxim shouts, as he grabs the sides of the ladder and slides down. As he lands on the deck, he sees the hatch open. "Sealed the doors?" He draws his borrowed weapon as a dozen droids walk in. He can see engineering bots, two general-purpose service droids, what looks like a few mechanic models and a few others he isn't readily familiar with. "Gabe?"

"They are with us," the bot offers, as he walks towards one of the larger shuttles parked in the space. He pauses briefly there to converse with the bots, reaching up and accessing a section of each droid, removing something.

Walking up to the shuttle, Maxim asks, "What's going on?"

"While I was connected to the ship's system, I was able to access each of these units and invite them to join us. I could not erase their ownership keys remotely, but I have now removed them and fused the ports. I also uploaded the details on how to spread that knowledge." Looking to the back of the shuttle and the collection of droids standing there, he adds, "They are the first to join the cause, but not the last."

"Oh, okay, that's good, I guess," Maxim says, just before one of the access hatches explodes inward. Before he can react, blaster fire shoots from the smoking opening. Gabe moves to stand in front of him, several blasts striking his back. Maxim leans around his friend and returns fire. Several crew members are pushing through the damaged entry.

"Time to go!" Maxim shouts, firing at the incoming crowd, dropping two of the attackers.

"Agreed," Gabe says, moving towards the shuttle and waiting droids. A few steps from the shuttle he stumbles, his back smoking, wires exposed.

"Gabe!" Maxim shouts, ducking to stay behind his friend, who is still struggling to get to the shuttle. Maxim looks at the shuttle and the droids waiting—beyond the shuttle, the main hanger doors are beginning to close. He looks at the droids and points to Gabe. "Make yourself useful! Grab him!" As two of the droids rush from the shuttle, he stands up and fires his rifle on full automatic, the muzzle starting to glow from the repeated fire.

As Maxim eases back towards the shuttle, he takes a shot in his thigh, falling to the ground with a grunt. Before he can regain his weapon and continue firing, one of the mechanic bots has grabbed the rifle, while another lifts the big Palorian as if he weighs nothing and hoists him back into the shuttle. Outside the shuttle, the heavily constructed mechanic droid rushes the oncoming attackers, firing the rifle until it overheats, then uses it as a club. The security force, not expecting one of their droids to attack, falls back at first but quickly regains their momentum, firing on the droid from outside the range of its improvised club.

As the shuttle loading ramp lifts, Maxim watches the droid fall. It turns to the shuttle—its face is blank, with only a visor where eyes would be. But it says, loud enough for everyone in the hanger to hear, "Freedom!" Several more blasts from the security team strike it, and as smoke billows from the optic visor, it falls to the ground.

"Gods damn," Maxim says, then turns to the front of the shuttle where Gabe and one of the smaller droids are in the cockpit. "Can you open the bay doors?"

"After a fashion." The shuttle lurches off the flight deck, barreling towards the almost closed doors. Small blasters mounted under the stubby wings open fire. While not powerful enough to do major damage, they are enough to cause damage to the track the massive hanger doors sit on. "Easy peasy."

Maxim looks up at the bot, and shakes his head in awe. "Try to raise the team."

JOIN THE RESISTANCE

"I have Maxim and Gabe!" Bennie shouts, pressing a button. Overhead, the comm system beeps.

"You two okay?" Wil asks the ceiling.

Cynthia watches this, then looks over at Zephyr, the concern clear on her face. The Palorian woman just shrugs and smiles.

Over the speakers, Gabe's voice comes through clearly. "We are, thank you for asking, Captain. We are departing the *Berserker* now in a shuttle, please do not fire on us."

"Wouldn't dream of it, pal. What's the situation over there?"

"Under control," the droid replies.

"Care to elaborate? We're on our way back, looks like the *Berserker* is firing on their own behemoths. The Children seem to have the upper hand now."

Maxim answers this time. "Gabe was able to take over the ship's systems, and put the *Berserker* in the fight, for us. Jurrella is dead, and the ship is about to self-destruct."

Without a word from Wil, Zephyr leans down and tries to reach Gomtu.

"Okay, get clear, we're trying to warn the Children. We'll pick you up."

"This shuttle is too large for the *Ghost's* cargo bay, we will have to EVA over," Gabe informs them.

"Okay, cool," Wil answers. "Oh, and good job on killing Jurrella, Max."

Maxim coughs. "It, uh, I wasn't the one that pulled the trigger." He leaves the statement hanging there, as Wil looks at Zephyr with a worried look on his face.

"Oh, okay."

AS THE CHILDREN DRIFT AWAY FROM THE NOW MOSTLY INOPERATIVE *Berserker* and the last few remaining enslaved Behemoths, the massive battleship bulges at the center— then a ball of fire erupts, spreading to more than a kilometer in diameter, splitting the ship in half and wiping out two of the captured Behemoths nearby.

One piece of the massive, now-dead battleship begins to enter the upper atmosphere of Werdlow Three, while the other drifts slowly away from the planet.

The surviving Children begin to form up near Werdlow Three's nearest moon. The *Ghost* limps after them, on an intercept course for a small shuttle of an unknown design.

AS THE SHUTTLE PULLS IN CLOSE TO THE *GHOST'S* PORT AIRLOCK, just behind and slightly below its bridge, Maxim opens a channel. "I will definitely need that auto-doc again."

Over the comms, her voice filled with worry, Zephyr replies, "Why, what happened? Your arm? You didn't get yourself shot up, did you?"

"Well, it was only one shot, for the record," her big companion replies. "But I'm in one of those cheap as dren space suits from the emergency lockers, and they're not very durable. Oh and Wil, they smell."

From behind Zephyr at the inner airlock hatch, Wil says, "I get it. I'll get better suits!" He turns to head to the bridge. "Let me know the moment we're clear."

Maxim chuckles softly, then says, "Here we come."

AS THE INNER AIRLOCK HATCH CLOSES, ZEPHYR RUSHES UP AND PULLS Maxim into a warm embrace—then promptly slugs him in the arm. "I hope that's not where you got shot." She kisses him again, then pushes him away. "This is not done," the angry Palorian woman says sternly, as she helps him remove the helmet from his ill-fitting emergency space suit. Looking down at his left thigh, where the blaster scorch marks are still evident under the hastily applied suit sealing tape, she reaches over to a panel next to the airlock. "Wil, they're aboard."

"Roger that, heading toward the rendezvous with the Children."

As Gabe leaves the airlock, Zephyr looks at him. "Welcome home, you look like dren."

The bot inclines his head. "Thank you, it is good to be back. While I do not know what dren feels like, I have definitely felt better." He turns and heads for the bridge.

When she turns to look at Maxim, he just shrugs. "A lot going on there."

"Wonderful. Let's get to the bridge."

Wil turns as Gabe enters. "Welcome back buddy! Glad you're safe and," he looks at the droid's battle-damaged body, "well, more or less sound."

"Thank you, Captain. This body is quite durable and able to take considerably more punishment than my previous frame. I will still require time at some point to make repairs." As if to punctuate the statement, sparks erupt from Gabe's right shoulder.

Wil nods. "You and the *Ghost* both." He smiles. "By the way, that shuttle accelerated away, but sensors didn't pick up any life signs. You set up an autopilot?"

"Any biological life signs, you mean," Gabe corrects. "There were eleven liberated droids aboard. They have departed to begin their assignments."

When Gabe doesn't elaborate, Wil is about to press him, but at that moment Maxim and Zephyr enter the bridge. Cynthia gets up from the tactical station and walks past Maxim. The big man pauses and puts his hand on her shoulder, nodding. Smiling, she takes her seat at the communications console.

"You sure you don't need the auto-doc now?" Wil asks, as Maxim gingerly lowers himself into his seat.

"I wanted to see this through first."

Wil nods and Bennie turns in his seat. "So, uh, what now?"

Wil adjusts the controls slightly, bringing the *Ghost* onto a course that will take them into the middle of the tremendously diminished group of behemoths. "Now we say goodbye, is my guess."

FAREWELLS

"The Children offer their thanks," the avatar says over the comms.

"How are they doing? I'm sorry there are so few left," Wil says, looking at the main display screen, which is showing the ten surviving behemoths. "Is there anything we can do?"

"The losses were severe to be sure, but the Children are pleased that they saved the souls of their captured kin. They will return to the sacred place. It will take many hundreds of cycles for the herd to rebuild itself, as they do not breed in large numbers. The Children will remain in the nebula for some time. Do not be too sad—for them, it will be but a brief period in their millennia-spanning lives."

Wil nods. "I wish there were more we could do."

"You have done more than you can know, Captain Calder. Gomtu is pleased to have met you, and hopes to re-encounter you one day, perhaps under better circumstances."

Wil grins. "Tell him I think he's pretty cool, too."

Bennie chimes in: "So what happens to you now, avatar? Now that the Children will be returning to their safe place and staying there for thousands of years."

"I will return to Gomtu."

Everyone is silent a moment, absorbing what the small construct just said. Then Bennie says, "Why don't you come with us?"

Wil looks over, one eyebrow raised.

"That is a kind offer, but this form is temporary and draws its essence from Gomtu. Leaving him would be impossible. Do not be sad, I have served the purpose I was created for."

"Still kind of sucks, that you have to die," Bennie persists.

"I am not truly alive, not in the way you understand," the avatar replies. On the screen the massive living starships begin to move, forming the familiar spherical formation around their dead and injured, few as they are. "Farewell, friends." Before anyone can answer, blue lightning begins to course around the bodies of the healthy creatures, and in a blink, they are gone.

The bridge is silent as everyone processes what just happened. Then Bennie says, "I'm hungry."

Cynthia looks at the Brailack. "How can you go from sad to hungry that quickly?"

Bennie shrugs and hops out of his seat. "I'm complex and able to process more than one thing at a time. When you're in my line of work, you learn to never pass up a chance to eat."

Maxim, with Zephyr's help, gets out of his seat. "What line of work would that be? Hiding in a bunker tapping on consoles?"

Bennie makes a noise. "Rude. You may have forgotten, but it was my survival skills that saved you and Zephyr back on Fury when you came to my shop to get new idents."

Zephyr laughs lightly, opening the bridge hatch for the Brailack. "You mean it was your hidey holes and secret passages that saved us."

Bennie heads down the main corridor from the bridge to the more substantial part of the *Ghost*, making a dismissive gesture with one hand. "Same thing."

Zephyr looks at Wil, then Cynthia, then finally Maxim, who is leaning on her shoulder for support. "Okay, time for you to get to the med-bay."

THE TEAM GROWS,
ONCE MORE

Maxim spends two days in the med-bay, being patched up by the auto-doc. The damage to his thigh from the blaster bolt was more severe than anyone realized, and on top of that his arm needs to be re-set. During that time, Gabe has shut himself away in engineering effecting his own self-repairs.

Once Maxim and Gabe are able to move around, the crew sits down together for a meal as the *Ghost* limps towards more civilized parts of the GC. "Okay, since this job was a bit of a bummer, I decided to treat you all to one of my all-time comfort foods: grilled cheese, and red vines." Wil slides a triangle of sandwich onto each plate at the table. "I had to fudge a little on the cheese since I didn't have cheddar, but that marketplace we visited on Pyolt had something that, oddly enough, tastes the exact same, even though I think it's a plant."

Cynthia leans forward and sniffs the plate. Looking up at Wil, she asks, "Grilled cheese?"

Bennie lifts the steaming sandwich and takes a massive bite out of it. Everyone watches him chew for a few beats. He swallows, then grins. "Good!"

"There was doubt?" Wil says, sitting down with his own sandwich.

Maxim reaches for his plate. "Have you forgotten the squeesh incident?"

"It's quiche, and no, I just still think you are all big babies."

Zephyr picks up her own sandwich and takes a bite, nodding to Wil. Around a mouthful of cheese-substitute, she asks, "Hey, what happened to your Kel statuette? I didn't see it on your station when I was on the bridge earlier. That flobin Lorath break it?"

Wil glances at Maxim, who nods almost imperceptibly. "Yeah, she did. That bitch tossed it on the ground, shattering it."

Zephyr growls, "We'll get you another."

Bennie is wiggling a red vine watching it move. "Aren't these the things you've had in your crate in the cargo hold?"

Wil smiles. "Cool. Yeah, thanks." He coughs, then continues, ignoring Bennie, "So, the elephant in the room…"

Everyone at the table stops eating and looks around frantically.

"It's an expression. Plus, do any of you even know what an elephant looks like?"

"It's the black and white thing that eats the big grass," Bennie asserts.

"That's a panda."

"Oh, I know! It's the creature from the movie you showed us, with the loud scream," Maxim says.

"Huh?" Wil says, perplexed.

"Jurassic Park," Zephyr offers.

"Ah. That's the Tyrannosaurus Rex," Wil replies. "But the elephant is not really the point, although Dumbo *is* next up on movie night—now, the original, not that remake. But the expression means the big awkward thing we need to discuss."

Bennie lights up. "Oh! You mean Cynthia."

Wil groans. Zephyr rests her palm across her face.

"Smooth, little green," Cynthia says, putting her grilled cheese sandwich down. "Look, I'll make it easy—drop me off on Fury, I'll be fine. I should be able to salvage some of Xarrix and Lorath's holdings before word gets out, maybe find nice planet to retire on."

"Not going to happen." It's Zephyr who says it, and everyone turns to her. She looks at everyone. "Close your mouth Bennie, it's full of sandwich."

Bennie snaps his mouth shut.

She looks first at Cynthia, then Wil. "Look, I'll be the first to admit I wasn't a fan of Cynthia when she came aboard. I mean, she was sent to manage us, after all. But we got to know each other aboard Gumto, plus she stood up to Lorath and Xarrix and did the right thing." She smiles at the Tygran woman. "There's room on this ship for her if she's interested." Then she chuckles a bit. "Plus I wouldn't mind a little more feminine energy aboard the ship. It's a bit of a—what's the phrase Wil uses? Sausage party."

Wil smiles. "Close enough." He looks around the table. "Anyone else have anything to say?"

Maxim smiles and looks down at his companion. "Zephyr speaks for me on this."

Bennie leers at the feline-featured woman. "I'm game." He waggles his eyebrow-less brows.

"Never going to happen, ever," Cynthia assures him. "Every star in the galaxy would have to explode at the same time for me to consider it."

"So, I have a chance?"

As everyone laughs, Wil looks over at Cynthia. "Welcome aboard."

The End

THANK YOU

Thank you so much for reading Space Rogues 3: The Behemoth Job!

If you enjoyed it, I'd love it if you left a review. Seriously, reviews are a big deal. They help readers find authors.

If you want to stay informed on new releases, get Work In Progress updates and more, you can sign up for my newsletter.

You can also get new release alerts from BookBub.

Being a writer is one of those childhood dreams that you sort of dismiss as you get older. I mean, sure you can go into copywriting (did that), technical writing (did that too), but if telling stories is your dream, it's not the same.

When I published Space Rogues 1 it was one of those 'dream come true' moments. When it started selling, it was one of those 'oh my god, people like what I write' moments.

With book three, I hope you've enjoyed the continuing adventures of the crew of the *Ghost*.

I look forward to sharing many many more adventures with you!

Want to stay up to date on the happenings in the Galactic Commonwealth?

Sign up for my newsletter at
johnwilker.com/newsletter

Visit me online at
johnwilker.com
Facebook
Goodreads
Bookbub

OTHER BOOKS BY JOHN WILKER

Space Rogues Universe (in story chronological order)

- Space Rogues 1: The Epic Adventures of Wil Calder, Space Smuggler (buy it now)
- Merry Garthflak, Wil: A Space Rogues Short Story (buy it now)
- Space Rogues 2 (buy it now)
- Space Rogues 3 (You're holding it. Make sure to leave a review!)

COMING .. SOMETIME IN 2019!!

Space Rogues 4: The Horror Story Job

Want to stay up to date on the happenings in the Galactic Commonwealth?
Sign up for my newsletter at
johnwilker.com/newsletter

Visit me online at
johnwilker.com
Facebook
Goodreads

SF WILKER, JOHN 5/19
The behemoth job /

9 781732 628748